Penelope Gilliatt is the author of novels, short stories, plays and criticism and has also written an opera libretto commissioned by the English National Opera. Her past works include *Sunday, Bloody Sunday* (the screenplay), *A State of Change* and *The Cutting Edge*. Her latest novel is *Mortal Matters*. These last two titles are also available from Abacus. Penelope Gilliatt divides her time between New York and England.

Also by Penelope Gilliatt in Abacus:

MORTAL MATTERS
THE CUTTING EDGE

Penelope Gilliatt

SPLENDID LIVES

First published in Great Britain by
Secker and Warburg Ltd 1977
Published in Abacus by
Sphere Books Ltd 1985
30–32 Gray's Inn Road, London WC1X 8JL
Copyright © Penelope Gilliatt 1972, 1973, 1974, 1975, 1976, 1977

Most of these stories first appeared in *The New Yorker*. 'Autumn of a
Dormouse' first appeared in the *Atlantic Monthly*; 'Phone-In' and 'A
Lovely Bit of Wood' in the *Transatlantic Review*. The stories are
published here with the editors' kind permission.

Set in 10/11 pt Garamond

Printed and bound in Great Britain by
Collins, Glasgow

To Tin

Contents

Splendid Lives

The Bishop of Hurlingham, aged ninety-two, radical, widowed, is a cousin three times removed of Queen Victoria and would not have troubled to endear himself to the royal mind, his own being well occupied with books, pigeons, politics, and worry at the moment over the self-imposed starvation diet of his beautiful Derby winner. And also – when he slept, fitfully, in his library – with thoughts of the Almighty, of his dead wife, of the blessings brought by the young, and of the noble father that begat him, whom he suspected of being more stoutly thoughtless than history recorded.

He sat this evening at the head of his illustrious family's oak table, this more than illustrious dissenter, and tried with native interest to create something cohesive of the three other people dining there. His younger sister, Biddy, aged eighty-six, sat facing him. Before the First World War, the Bishop had chained himself to the railings of the Houses of Parliament with her and his wife, and been sent with the suffragettes to prison, where he had joined their hunger strikes.

A local ear, nose, and throat specialist on his left, Dr Spencer, had been trying for years to get him to his office for treatment for deafness. 'Come on Tuesday and we'll play a rubber of bridge afterwards,' Dr Spencer said to him loudly. 'Apart from that, there is a question of your hearing. The treatment I'd like you to have admittedly went out quite widely between the two world wars, but it's still the best.'

'Oh,' said the Bishop, staring at the foot of the table and missing his wife. 'Is that so? What does it involve?'

'Copper wires.'

'I don't hear you.'

'Copper wires.'

'That's what I thought you said.'

'Through the nose and out of the ears. Thin as a moth's antenna.'

'What's that you say about moths? I got the rest.'

'No alarm,' said Dr Spencer.

Ridgeway, the American girl on the Bishop's right, shivered.

'You don't say,' said the Bishop. He bent his head courteously towards Dr Spencer and at the same time gave a push to a modern

1

chrome trolley bearing plates of consommé in the direction of Ridgeway, a pretty, long-haired revolutionary girl whom he had sat down with in Trafalgar Square in a demonstration about Rhodesia.

'It was good of you to protest about Southern Rhodesia,' the Bishop said to her. 'Our government's behaviour hasn't been your fault.'

'Certainly not yours,' said Ridgeway.

'But I'm afraid one still tends to think in terms of countries,' said the Bishop. 'I hesitated about protesting against Vietnam in public, for example. I thought our own house had better be put in order first. Which requires a certain amount of nippiness in revolt by the English.'

Biddy said, 'I remember your wife once saying that any society that depresses free meddling is on the decline, however flamboyant its immediate spoils. The idea stuck in my mind. She said it when we were chained to Downing Street.'

'Really a good treatment for him?' Ridgeway asked Dr Spencer.

'I fancy copper wires would bring back to you the days of forcible feeding, dear Biddy,' said the Bishop, who had also undergone it in prison in 1912 and who had been one of the only men to risk ridicule from other men in clubs and Parliament for his position. 'Barbarous. And the doctors who did it wouldn't even take their hats off in the presence of a lady when they were in her cell. That annoyed some suffragettes as much as the error of the procedure, though I privately think anyone who objected then about etiquette was being a bit of an ass. In fact, I thought complaining over politesse as well as over politics was wanting to have it both ways, though everyone is entitled to invent his or her own peccadilloes. One of the things I like about America is that when it makes a moral mess of things it really makes an *unholy* mess. I must admit there have been times when I have felt on the verge of despair about us all.'

The Bishop addressed himself to Ridgeway and congratulated her on keeping her swinging hair out of the soup. Conversation then ran into the sand. The Bishop restored things, as he generally did. 'Well, let's plough on. Give the trolley a shove to my sister, would you be so good?' he said to Ridgeway, as it came to her for a second helping. 'You'll have to take care it doesn't slop, being consommé.'

'My brother's wife had an amiable cook who asked once if she wanted the consommé thick or clear,' Biddy shouted.

'No need to yell for my sake, dear,' said the Bishop, whose own voice was soft. 'You don't mind our using the trolley, do you?'

2

he said to Ridgeway. 'It saves walking about for the butler and valet. For Wren, I mean. He got a nasty hit in a leg in the war and they didn't get all the shrapnel out. He's politically on the left, like the rest of us. He told me yesterday he got on with you. You were the first American he'd met, he said, apart from the Catholic Cardinal of New York, whom we were obliged to entertain when my wife was alive. The Cardinal and I found no difficulties between us apart from this question of Christianity's link with capitalism. I am afraid it is a question that has somewhat driven me away from Church dogma, though not from speculation, I hope. It is only in this matter that thought has caused disappointment.'

'Not your age?' Dr Spencer asked.

'By George, age doesn't blight the fun. To go back, it has begun to seem to me all too possible that the great sin of capitalism – apart from usury, greed, exploitation, and so forth – may well be kin to the great sin of the Christian Church when the schisms set in. Capitalism in practice inclines to splits. So in Western capitalism, as in Western Christianity, we have created a magnificent theoretical ethic of the majority, but it is a majority that no one feels part of.'

'We did in Trafalgar Square,' Ridgeway said.

'No, I'm afraid we were no more than a handful of the whole. It was good of you to turn up. One looks to foreigners for help. I noticed at the time what pretty ankles you had.'

'And her political opinions?' said Biddy kindly.

'First-rate, I should say. Yes! Yes! The scent of new ideas is very fascinating. Keep shoving the trolley round, Biddy. You'll find you can avoid the grated carrots if you're thinking of another plateful.' He turned to Ridgeway. 'The war, the Second World War, turned us rather against carrots. Lord Woolton, who was the Minister of Food of the time, was very keen on root vegetables because the English could grow them in their gardens and allotments and so on. One might say he pushed carrots. They were said to be good for the eyesight of pilots, so we ate them in every form – carrot soufflé, carrot devil's-food cake – though none of the immediate family was a pilot. They also improved the possibility of seeing in the blackout, which of course we all had to do. My personal suspicion is that his carrot propaganda was apocryphal, wouldn't you say? A way of filling us up,' he said, turning to Dr Spencer.

'I was rather young at the time,' Dr Spencer said.

'Stupid of me. All the same, it's history, therefore still with us.' The Bishop took the crust off a piece of bread and ate the middle.

'Back to Lord Woolton, who wasn't such a humourless soul as he seemed by any means; you might say he had quite a visionary approach to root vegetables in general. We all got rather bored with advertisements in the papers for a character called Potato Pete, who was drawn with the face of an unpeeled potato and who would appear over potato recipes. I look much like Potato Pete myself. It struck me while shaving the other day.'

His sister studied him. 'Potato Pete didn't have bristly eyebrows and he didn't laugh as much as you, though I'm blessed if I can often see what you find to laugh about.'

'Well, Biddy, there's the rest of the world, which accumulates surprise and buffoonery as one grows older, and there are certain cheering steps forward here and there, and books that have an exact comic sense of folly: quite a lot of them new. And there's Bucephalus,' he went on to Ridgeway, 'our quixotic genius of a horse, whose mind is more and more interesting to get to the bottom of. And then there's this pleasant place, where one could hardly feel got down. Ah, pie.'

Another trolley had been brought to Ridgeway's left by Wren. 'Is it quail pie?' asked the Bishop, looking at the dish on the Georgian tray.

'Yes, My Lord,' said Wren.

'What do you like to be called?' Ridgeway asked.

'Well, you try "My Lord", but I don't really care for it much in conversation, do you? It's a bit of a boulder. That leaves "Dr Hurlingham" or "Bishop". Is "Bishop" rather burdensome? My Christian name is Paul. I wish I could say that I had had a visitation anything up to his, but you could hardly reduce me to Saul when it was not the name my parents hoped for, could you? In modern times, that name anyway belongs to the young man who does those brilliant screen credits, wouldn't you say?'

'You mean Saul Bass? How do you know about him?' Ridgeway asked.

'Oh, he's very well known, isn't he? Full of life. Lovely work. Poor girl,' he said, looking at her dealing with the thing on the silver monarchial tray. 'Quail pie is always a problem. You've just stuck a fork into a second bird, haven't you? It's a question of judging the width of any particular quail you're after, but I'm bothered if I can see how you can do that when you don't know where the edge of it is. The crust should have been cut in the kitchen.'

Ridgeway had used up three forks by now and each time hit a quail, and to lift out the forks would have ruined the entire pastry

4

crust. The pie looked like a bull near the end of a bullfight: on its knees.

'The thing is to use a knife and get under the pastry crust to have a look,' said the Bishop. Ridgeway did.

Now well dismembered, the pie on its trolley with three vegetables and bread sauce continued round via the two women to Dr Spencer. The Bishop said, 'You won't mind if I skip the pie and concentrate on the other thing? At my age, it's more trouble than it's worth, and there's plenty of pleasure in mashed potatoes and bread sauce.'

'And in gravy,' Ridgeway said.

'I'm sure we could get those teeth on their legs again,' said Dr Spencer.

'On their *legs?*' said the Bishop, laughing till his eyes poured tears and dabbing them with a beautiful lawn handkerchief. 'Oh dear, the tricks that language can play. The poor Pope was praying for peace at the United Nations and was reported in translation as saying that he hoped the nations of the world would let their arms fall from their hands. It made me wish I could draw.' He took out a felt pen and did a cartoon on the back of his cheese plate.

'You can do almost anything, dear,' said Biddy.

'Well, it's a question of setting your mind to it. Though I've certainly set my mind to getting Bucephalus to eat for the next season and he won't touch a thing. My late wife could always get him to eat before a big race.' The Bishop went on thinking of the shapely Derby winner off his feed in the stables.

'You'll excuse me if I don't stay for the pudding,' Hurlingham said, getting up. 'I foresee junket. The cook makes it for me every evening on account of the tooth problem but I can never touch it. Bucephalus and I may have something in common. I thought for a time that Wren, who has remarkable powers of observation, had hit on it. He noticed that the horse would only eat when a pigeon was in the loose box. The pigeon would generally sit on the horse's back. Then the pigeon died. Disaster for Bucephalus. Nutritionally speaking. Skin and bones. A pitiful sight. So Wren got another pigeon and the horse seemed to take to him well enough, but the oats were still untouched . . . You'll excuse me? You've scarcely begun your sherry,' he said to Dr Spencer. 'It's left in the drawing-room.'

'I'm afraid I was late,' said Dr Spencer.

'Calls, I daresay.'

'No, traffic.'

'It's the cars that slow things up now. The anger. This is no time for hostility. It tends to have a leadening effect, don't you find?'

he said to Ridgeway. He got up by himself to wander along the immense corridor, down the curling back stairway to the stables, and gazed at the beautiful horse. It gazed back, food untouched.

'He hasn't had his cream cheese, either,' said Biddy, still in the dining-room and looking at her brother's place. 'If you could only get him in shape to enjoy summer pudding again, Dr Spencer.'

'What's summer pudding?' Ridgeway asked.

'It was always his favourite, even in the nursery. Mostly a matter of white bread and fresh raspberries. But the pips give him trouble now.'

'I shouldn't say it's entirely his bite,' said Dr Spencer. 'It may be that he has something on his mind. He misses his wife, doesn't he?'

'Even after six years. Yes, I remark on it to myself all the time and wonder what to do. A pretty girl with a well-read mind perks him up,' Biddy said to Ridgeway. 'I was noticing him with you.'

'I'm too slow for him, though. Do you mind if I go to bed?' said Ridgeway. 'I'm too tired even to read.'

'The sloth of youth, the energy of age,' said Biddy after she had gone, rolling up her dinner napkin into a cylinder for her napkin ring and then doing the same for Ridgeway's. 'That girl is very good for him. I don't think she's encountered a linen napkin before.'

'I don't believe she knew how to get it into the napkin ring,' Dr Spencer said. 'Or perhaps she abandoned things because she was expecting a clean napkin for breakfast. Americans have clean napkins at every meal.'

'My goodness the laundering that must go on! The starching! The ironing! Why a fresh one every time? It's not as if she wore lipstick. In the twenties, when we all did, of course, one's napkin was often a wreck after dinner. It was a problem to eat asparagus and artichokes successfully without getting jammy around the mouth. And one would never have repaired make-up at the table as girls do now.'

'He's a remarkable man for his years,' said Dr Spencer. 'You shouldn't worry about him. His age doesn't seem to be doing any harm to his sense of curiosity, or indeed his rebelliousness.'

'No, it's not,' said Biddy. 'A life needs weight in its tail, you see.' She paused for a while. 'The only great drawback for him is missing his wife, but he doesn't let it affect him. In fact, I've often noticed that someone's sense of option and possibility even grows when most has apparently been whittled away.'

✢

Ridgeway found her way to the stable yard and saw the Bishop leaning over the bottom of the loose box. The horse's beautiful head tossed up at the sight of a stranger and then settled back to watch the Bishop. The pigeon pecked at the oats and didn't look at the horse.

'I was thinking of writing a biography of that horse,' said the Bishop. Three English sheepdogs stood beside him on the cobbles, balancing on their hind legs and reaching just high enough to rest their muzzles on the bottom half of the door. 'When I woke up this morning, I found I had the article all planned. It would be poor of me not to do it. The things I have missed doing are vexing thoughts.'

'A biography of a *horse*?' Ridgeway said.

'Yes. It would seem to me not in the least mad, though there is something essential I still haven't hit on about Bucephalus' turn of thought. Anyway, why not a horse? A most interesting, noble and innovative life, this one's. You have wonderfully pretty legs.'

Ridgeway looked down at them.

'Would you like a holiday job as the sheepdogs' walker?' the Bishop asked. 'They don't get enough amusement.'

Ridgeway went on considering her legs. 'Good legs or not, they don't necessarily make me a good walker,' she said.

'No, but I have the feeling . . . Brood about it.'

In the meantime, he thought about her legs, the pigeon, and his hungry, enthralling horse. 'Naturally, it would be a test to do the article well enough.'

'If it were vivacious, you mean you'd be on your way to it?'

'That would be essential. It always is. Ridgeway, what could be more puzzling than a Derby winner who so misses a pigeon that he's starving himself to death? Company, is that the secret? What's unsatisfactory about *this* pigeon?' He laughed, and his steel-wool eyebrows shot up. Then he said soberly to Ridgeway, 'What are you laughing about?'

'Your gaiters, the pigeon, the horse, the mud.'

'Oh, yes, it is muddy, isn't it?' He had a torch in his hand that he lowered to the level of his own legs little though they interested him. 'You see, I should like to do this biography adequately.' He flashed his torch at her left hand. 'Aren't you married? You live with someone in America, I expect.'

'I'm getting divorced, I'm afraid.'

'I daresay you're right. Why?'

'He was a banker, and I wasn't old enough until the last moment to know that I didn't like what he did.' She paused.

'What did you discover?' said the old man, shaking his head.

'What difference does it make? Wouldn't it be boring to hear about?'

'No.'

'He hadn't much idea of what was happening. Of consequences, let alone causes. He couldn't see himself.'

'To leave an imprint somewhere by making the right snap decision, is that what was missing?'

'One spring we were on holiday in the West Indies and we bought a very good landscape by a young local painter. I was thrilled. And then my husband asked the painter if a bank could be put into the composition, and the painter gave him a look and painted in a bank in five minutes. He needed the money.'

'I may be wrong, but I think your generation and country express themselves most fully in immediate behaviour,' the Bishop said. 'Other times, other places do it through sculpture or writing. It is a question . . . Ah, suddenly I have it about the pigeon; it's the wrong *sex,* of course. It is a question whether we have ever seen the really vivid expression of a nation's temperament except on a plane of' – she thought he was going to say 'religion' – 'of art. In actions, we have hardly ever seen it. And religion has grown too confused with persuasion and prosperity. You know, of course, about the nineteenth-century offshoots that actually considered prosperity an attribute of God and made their followers feel shame for not reflecting it. It is also a pity that there is very little private prayer.'

A stable clock chimed. The Bishop said to himself, 'A *female* pigeon, a *female* pigeon, like the one that died.'

'You miss your wife.'

'Yes.'

'I'm afraid I don't miss my husband.'

'What was wrong with him, to your mind?'

'His boredom.'

The Bishop hesitated. 'I don't often talk about this, but I had a brother who died by playing hazard, and I think he did it in war against boredom.'

'How old was he?'

'Seventeen.'

'Young to be bored.'

'On, no, on the contrary, things become more interesting as you get older. For instance, the case of this horse and this pigeon. If my brother had waited, I believe he would have grown interested in things. The nature of his thinking was too flat and stale for him to bear at the time of the accident's happening, you see. But later it would have altered.'

'Do you look on suicide as a sin?'

'On, never mind about that now. Are you cold? I say, I am glad we hit on the idea of female pigeon.'

'You do distribute ideas. You thought of it.'

'Did I? I must dust the mud off my gaiters if you are going to be perceptive.'

'And he risked himself to get back the taste of things?'

'I was rather young, but I fancy he thought he could recover the savour of life by chancing the loss of it. He played Russian roulette by jaywalking just in front of a racing carriage. People nowadays find the tale picturesque. He deliberately stepped off the pavement in front of a carriage that was being driven very fast. You didn't do that, did you? When you and your husband agreed to get divorced?'

'When I decided to get married, perhaps?'

'Of course, people are at a disadvantage when they are dealing with anyone like your husband, to whom the idea of retreat is not a humiliation but a piece of strategy. I'm not speaking of your own nature but your position. I wonder if I could do a noble article about a horse. It should be possible. George Stubbs, now, his anatomical drawings of owls and so on had nobility.'

'It's not what people expect of you.'

'But therefore not a bad rebellion, in its small way. Neither of us can protest in Trafalgar Square all the time.'

They moved towards the house after the Bishop had patted the horse's head and felt his ribs.

'No lustre,' he said about the horse, his own eyes shining excitedly with ideas in the light thrown by the stable tower. 'I wish you would be a dog walker, but I can see you wouldn't meet many people.' Then he recognised the absurdity of what he had said, and picked her up and carried her over the mud. 'You must be careful of your frocks,' he said.

'I like that word,' she said. 'It's the first time I haven't worn jeans for ages.'

'I like jeans, too.'

'Pagan gaiters,' said Ridgeway.

'I like them in Trafalgar Square, at least. Or for picknicking, or painting, or mucking out stables.

'You were saying something about justified rebellion. Is there any such thing as justified war?'

'What do you think?' he said, still carrying her, his feet stumbling over the cobbles and his mind visibly teeming to hear her reply.

'I believe the war against the Nazis was. I don't think the Crusades were.'

'That's what I think. Now, the independence of India, the independence of Ulster, these are difficult questions. The thing would have been never to have behaved greedily in the first place.'

In the following week the male pigeon was replaced by a friendly female. The horse ate and had a spectacular season. The popular papers disapproved of a Bishop who owned a racehorse, especially a winning one. The serious gossip columns ran short paragraphs saying that he sent his winnings to Black Africa. The Bishop wrote finely about his horse. Ridgeway went to prison briefly for making another and more violent protest about Rhodesia, after sitting next to a middle-aged white woman liberal from Rhodesia who had told her about a four-foot cell for black dissidents who were found dead after days without water. Their footprints were on the ceiling, perhaps because of the need to keep walking somewhere. With a finger dipped in dirt, one of them had written in shaky capitals on the wall: 'HELLO OUT THERE.' The signal had been inscribed by a man whom the woman liberal had taught to write English after she had herself learned Shona.

Ridgeway's memory of the Bishop, the stable yard, the horse, the pigeon, the dark, her sense of her own weight when the old man was lifting her, recurred and recurred.

'Are you against violence?' she had said as he was carrying her. 'I'm a pacifist.'

He had stood still to think about it carefully. 'I am in general, too. I can see the possibility of violence being the only way to be gentle in the end. The difficulty is to be certain who is planning the violence and whether a gentle society is going to emerge from it. Most guerillas are too disorganized.' She was draped across his arms as if he were carrying a bridal dress stiffened with age. 'Is that your shoulder blade or my watch-strap?' he had said. 'Either way, it must be painful for you. We're only a minute from the steps. I'm afraid I'm a bit of a slow stroller now when I'm carrying a girl.'

'Am I heavy?' she had asked.

'No. I was just enjoying our conversation. I hadn't really noticed your lightness, which is rude of me, isn't it? You'll find the old do that. One gathers the mind to a point and the other things pass one by. It's a great blessing, age. There's more time.'

Fleeced

On a tropical island widely thought to be halcyon but harbouring the ires and envies of most small islands climatically blessed but socially consigned to rage, a small English boy by the name of Tom, aged ten, went swimming every morning before having breakfast of flying fish with his tutor, who would have preferred kippers.

The tutor, named Lionel, was Tom's absent father's accountant. He was a spider-shaped man who seemed born to wear black. Perhaps he had been christened in black: a lean babe, in mourning for a mistake in the ledgers, too troubled by the instability of sterling to waste tears over any anointment at the font. His adult being had a lined face, a chin like an infant's elbow, rosy lips, and an unchangeably indoor skin that suffered from the sun. At weekends he expressed a sense of spree by wearing flowered Hawaiian shirts, but on office days he wore the bowler hat and black suit that seemed native to him. It was always the same black suit, which looked rusty, like historic lead piping. He generally wore the floppy tropical shirts to give Tom his lessons, which were mostly in mathematics and in geography about Malaysia, where Lionel had fought in the war. His employer was a rich Englishman called David Lippincott, who had lately made his first million in the manufacture of tights and the selling of plays that had been put on at English repertory theatres to American movie corporations. Mr Lippincott profited very little from the film sales, but they eased his heart.

'And where is your husband?' said a bearded gossip reporter to Mrs Lippincott in London.

'As you know, we're separated.' Mrs Lippincott was a natural blonde called Andrea, even richer than her husband because she had inherited a fortune in a chain fishmongery.

'But where is he?'

'I think he's somewhere in America.'

'He left England?'

'That's what I said.'

'Why?'

'Perhaps because of me. He said it was because of the wealth tax.'

'And where is the son?'

'Our son?'

'The judge gave the father custody, of course, so I realize you may not know. And I realize these questions may be painful for you to face, but I'm only doing my job.'

Andrea looked as if she were likely to cry.

'I can't stand people crying,' said the reporter.

'I'm sorry,' said Andrea. She did her hair, leaning over to brush it so that it covered her eyes. 'Does crying happen a lot when you catechize people like this? Why do you do it? I can see you don't enjoy it.'

'I started as a cricket reporter. The paper promoted me to gossip because I have the fluency. The style. It's the nerve I'm not good at. You need very good nerves to be a first-rate gossip reporter. Whereas I have to brace myself in the morning even to get up. I mean, I don't look forward –' The reporter put his hands in his pockets, stopped speaking for a moment, and then said in a changed tone, 'Well, where *is* the son?'

'With his tutor. You don't expect me to give you his address, do you? He's a child.'

'You said your husband had to leave England because of the wealth tax?'

'I let that slip. That's his business. I don't know.'

'I see his Belgravia flat is up for sale.'

'He had to leave his flat and our son.'

'You used that order. I have it down. First you said "his flat" and then "his son."'

'Our son.'

'But you're not with the son. It's hardly a mother's instinct.'

'I work. I can't be.'

'What do you do in an average day?'

'Is it any business of yours?'

'You're in the public domain.'

'I get up at six. I have a bath. I do the post. My secretary comes. We do more post. Then I go to the central office. Then there's a business lunch. Do we need to go on?'

'You go often to South Africa?'

'My business takes me there.'

'But not to the son? He's in the Caribbean, isn't he? A long way from South Africa.'

'My husband has custody, as you said.' She did her hair again.

'Because of your visits to South Africa? Whom do you go to see?'

'I naturally have friends there.'

'Do I hear wedding bells?'

Andrea parted her hair and looked at him. 'Come off it.'

The reporter laughed uncertainly. 'I've got three kids and a mortgage. Could you at least tell readers what your imaginary ideal day would be?'

'Swimming before breakfast with Tom, and chocolate layer cake.'

On the tropical island, Lionel had his flying fish and Tom read.

After a while, Tom said, 'What are you going to do today? You're not going to be out too long? Perhaps we could do some calculus?'

'What's your imaginary favourite day?'

'Swimming. Then reading at breakfast. Then calculus. You don't like calculus, do you? In spite of your being an accountant?'

'You're dripping sea-water onto your book,' said Lionel. 'You'll spoil the binding. Not that a fine binding has much chance against this climate.'

'I know you don't like these particular tropics,' said Tom. 'But Malaysia's still your favourite subject in geography, isn't it? On account of having been there?'

'Yes. And what would happen after calculus?'

'I'd go for another swim, and then think about maths, and then wait for you to come home and perhaps there'd be a letter from my parents. One or the other of them.'

'As I told you, they're very busy.'

'Why are we here without my father?'

The telephone went.

'I thought you said the telephone didn't work,' said Tom.

'It must be the local operator.'

'That doesn't make sense.'

'Operators have ways,' said Lionel, trying to sound vague, though it was not his manner. 'I expect they're telling us the electricity is going off again. Everything in the refrigerator will be de-frozen. I'll have to pitch it all out. Nothing works here.'

'My mother once said you were a fuss-pot. I expect she only said it because my father had upset her. Is fuss-pot rude?'

'Well,' said Lionel, 'I expect it's true. I expect that's why your father hired me as his accountant.'

'I thought you were my tutor. That's what it says on your passport.'

'I'm here to look after your father's money, between ourselves, as well as you.'

'Why don't you do that in England?'

'What would be the rest of your favourite day?' said Lionel.

'Christmas pudding, and then chocolate *soufflé*, and then snorkling with you, and then a ride through the sugar canes if you aren't too tired, which I know you often are, and then steak and kidney pudding and smoked trout with my father, and then Monopoly with my father and whoever he liked at the moment. Susan, say. Or better still,' politely, 'my father and Susan *and* you. Or just you, if he's gone off to a nightclub with Susan.'

'I had a letter from your father saying you should have more pocket money.'

'Could I see it?'

'You're dripping marmalade on Thackeray. The letter's at the office.'

'You always keep his letters at the office. Couldn't I see them? He's my father. Couldn't I ring him?'

'I've told you often that the telephone here doesn't function further afield than the island. The lines are very bad in the tropics. Anyway, it would be prohibitively expensive. We have to look after the way your father's money goes.'

'Hell!' Tom reached into his pocket and threw a bunch of coins into the sea.

'It's time we did some work. I'll set you some problems before I go to the office,' said Lionel unsteadily.

Lionel prepared a set of questions for the child and shaved. Tom did them sitting in the sun, shading his eyes against the glare. Lionel had once offered him a sun hat but Tom had shaken his head. His bony knees were burnt and his collarbones had caught the sun yesterday, but his back had long since turned a painless deep brown, to his pride. He felt pity for Lionel in his floppy-sleeved Hawaiian shirt and long shorts, with his pale freckled calves that the sun did nothing to colour.

'I'm afraid I've nearly finished these questions,' he said to Lionel politely, when his tutor reappeared after shaving.

'That's too quick.'

'The heat makes my mind go faster. It boils my head.'

'Work through the questions again.'

'Shouldn't you change into your dark suit if you're going to the office? You're not by any chance taking a holiday?'

Lionel said, 'I'm afraid it's not possible. I'm just about to change.' Pause. 'If you'll put on your jacket I'll take you out to lunch today.'

'And show me the office?'

'The office is very boring.'

'But it's where my father once flew from America to see you,

you said. You said it when I was a small boy. You said the flight came in when I was asleep.'

'He doesn't come any longer. That would have been in the old days, before the tax laws were so strict.'

'What are we doing here?'

'I'm looking after your father's *money*. I've *explained* that to you. It isn't that he doesn't *want* to see you.'

'Why can't he look after his own money?'

'The money has to be here, and he has to be somewhere else, or else he'd have to pay so much of it in tax he wouldn't be able to look after you.'

'But he isn't looking after me. How can he, when he isn't here?'

'I'm here instead, teaching you. I'm sorry. It's not enough, is it? But there's also the swimming, and the snorkling.' Lionel blew his nose with a beautiful lawn handkerchief.

'What would be *your* favourite day?' said Tom.

'Well. I like trains. English trains. I like routine.'

'There aren't any trains here.'

'Waterloo Bridge in the rush hour!' said Lionel at speed: speaking to himself, it seemed, lying back on a deck-chair with an old copy of *The Economist* on his knees to protect his legs from the sun. 'The *Financial Times* on the day it comes out! Lunch in the City! Secretaries who know how to take shorthand instead of these girls!' He spoke faster, with fervour. 'Oh, the rush of it! Telephones! Closing prices on the Stock Exchange! I'm being overpaid here, you know.' He slowed down. 'It's what they call a sinecure. I'm just here to give a name to your father's account, between ourselves. There's nothing to the job, I fear.'

'Then why doesn't my father do it?'

'It would mean his taking up residence here. Your father's a busy man. He hasn't got the time. I do the residing for him.'

Tom killed a wasp.

'And then what would your favourite evening be?' Tom said. 'Supposing you got home about 4 o'clock?'

'I might go snorkling with you. And then I'd have a few business friends over to play George Gershwin records. I don't think you know that my sister and I used to have everything that George Gershwin ever recorded.'

'You've never mentioned your sister.'

'She's in Australia.'

'How bloody awful.'

'Don't say bloody.'

'Well, but it is.'

'I can't say I don't miss her, especially when I hear music.'

'Any music?'

'Yes.' Pause.

'Then what would you have for supper? Or would it be dinner?'

'It would be dinner. You'd be there. Either beef steak and kidney pie, or gammon and pease pudding, and then a spot of Wensleydale with a decanter of port. The best port. Cockburn's, I dare say. Wensleydale is a sort of cheese. I expect you've forgotten it. Perhaps you've never had it. We can't get it here.'

'I'm sure my father and mother gave it to me before the break-up.'

'I'm sure they did,' said Lionel, turning away to look at the bright sea.

The telephone rang again. Lionel sighed, went in to answer it this time, and yelled, 'Please call me at the office, sir.' Then Tom heard him recant and say that he would talk here for once if it was so urgent. The boy blocked his ears with wads of bread, frightened of something he couldn't name to himself. He could still hear, unfortunately. He tried to get interested in using a calculator to work out the *Financial Times*.

'Argentinian pesos into Swiss francs, forty thousand pounds sterling! Right sir!' shouted Lionel. Tom was about to rush in to say, 'No, buy Brazilian cruzeiros,' when he realized with absolute certainty that Lionel was speaking to his father and that his father was not going to speak to him. He pressed his knees together. The bones had made red marks on the skin by the time the conversation finished.

'That was father, wasn't it?' said Tom when Lionel came out again onto the terrace through a hanging door of coloured beads. Men had arrived to clean out the swimming pool and it was slowly draining.

'His New York office,' said Lionel kindly, though not deceiving Tom. 'If it had been him he'd naturally have wanted to speak to you.'

'You told me you couldn't get overseas calls here.'

'It must have been a fluke. Do you want to try to get your mother? One fluke can lead to another.'

Tom threw his lessons down the cliff into the sea.

'Homesickness is a bad business,' said Lionel, watching the papers slowly submerge.

'I'm not homesick, I'm just sick of being parked.'

'There's lunch for us to look forward to. I thought we could go to a men's club that I like.'

'Would my father be paying?' Tom asked, with his back turned.

'Why?'

'It sounds expensive. You're not rich like him, too, are you? I hate rich people.'

'No, I'm not, but I've got plenty for a treat.' Lionel watched Tom's back. 'You mustn't forget he's doing it all for you. Would you sign this cheque?'

'What are these cheques I sign every week?'

'Your father's allowance. He's a limited company. You're the director.'

'I'd rather we were all together and poor instead. We could live on sausage rolls.'

A 50p English coin spilled out of Lionel's pocket when he drew out his handkerchief to blow his nose again. Tom picked it up and said joyfully, 'It's English.'

'It used to take the form of four half-crowns,' said Lionel.

'I know,' said Tom. 'I've read about half-crowns.'

Lionel blew his nose yet again.

'What's the matter? You only usually blow your nose once after breakfast,' said Tom.

'It sounded as if you were talking about something as gone as the groat,' said Lionel. 'Even the guinea is done with.'

'We miss England, don't we?'

'Yes. Though that's a foolish thing for me to say to you when you're of an age to be looking forward to the future. I don't like catching myself hankering.'

'Did you have a bad night?'

Lionel sat down with his flowered sleeves flapping and looked out to sea. 'I dreamt that the surface of the Earth was green and glassy, covered with shattered elements.'

Lionel dressed for the office. He set some more questions for Tom and arranged for the chauffeur to drive the boy into the island's little capital for lunch. Tom cleaned Lionel's black City shoes.

'You need to use the polish sparingly,' said Lionel.

'What's sparingly?' asked Tom. 'A little or a lot?'

Lionel suddenly shouted at him. 'I'm not a nanny! I'm an accountant!'

Tom remained silent, and then said, 'More difficult than the work, I expect, is being shut up with me.'

'That's the best part. You're what we call a perk, in City talk.' Then, 'I shouldn't have shouted. I had no right. Your father's very good to me.'

Tom thought, and then said, 'I think the trouble is you and me not having time off together. You're always working.'

'So are you. And at the same subject. You doing calculus at

home, me doing accounts at the office.'

'I enjoy it more than you do. Could I borrow your calculator?'

'As long as we're on time for lunch. When one makes an appointment it's upsetting if it isn't abided by. You know my rule for happiness? Keep the mind busy and the body seated. I realize it wouldn't be a rule to suit you, and it's better fitted to the City of London than to a tropical paradise.'

Tom heard the bitterness in his friend's voice, was wounded by it, and wondered what to do about it. 'Your City suit's getting old,' he said, watching Lionel leave in the chauffeur-driven car.

'I can't quite afford another one. It doesn't matter.'

'My father would pay.'

Lionel was silent.

'Wouldn't he?'

'I must go off. I've got something difficult to do for your father.'

'About the pesos?'

'What pesos? Get your lessons done. Will you wear your grey flannel suit for lunch?'

Lionel was not a very speedy-minded accountant. He often had daymares about failing in his responsibility for the dual guardianship of Tom and of the tropical bank account. Within half an hour Tom had finished all the other lessons he could manage on his own; he spent the rest of the time working out theoretical financial exchanges.

Lionel secreted a vein of boyishness and dash that was not hidden from Tom. The boy remembered well that, when the black suit had been newer, Lionel had come into the London house with some papers and explained his black tie to Mrs Lippincott: 'I had to go to the funeral of a cousin yesterday – no, to be precise, a second cousin once removed – and it turned out to be quite jolly. We went on after the service and lunched, a very cordial lunch, and I saw many people I hadn't met for years. There were no hostiles there, you see.' Lionel used 'hostiles' as a noun. Tom liked his language.

The boy arrived a little early at the men's club where they were lunching. It was raining. Tom's suit was damp. He saw that Lionel's was damper.

'Are you going to get pneumomia?' said Tom.

'No, not a scrap or scintilla of illness shall invade our domain. It's not really raining. I mean, one would be glad of a mac, but one doesn't necessarily need a brolly.'

Many people other than Tom would meet Lionel and come

away augustly sobered, and then find that the bequest of his company was one of both precision and blitheness. He spoke to Tom as if to an adult, perhaps because he remembered so exactly what it is to be a child, and because he perpetually felt himself a ten-year-old who happened to be walled up in an adult carcase.

The club was nominally de-segregated, and blacks were welcome enough at business lunches. In other cases the management would often find some means of turning blacks away: a technicality about dress, no admission to members' guests who were not themselves members. As Lionel and Tom were waiting in the foyer, a young black couple whose wish for lunch obviously had nothing to do with business and everything to do with being in love were turned away at the desk.

'I'm afraid Madam isn't a member,' said the manager. 'I regret.'

'She's my guest,' said the young man. The girl held on to his arm.

'We can't permit non-members.' The manager busied himself with something behind a grille.

The girl twisted her engagement ring. The man swore wildly for some minutes. Then the girl said in a quiet voice to the manager's silhouette, 'You are not wise.' The couple left.

At lunch, Lionel knew Tom was re-enacting what had gone on. 'The girl did well,' Lionel said. 'One doesn't have to say or do many things, but one has to be careful to say and do the right things. There are times in history that may require a rejoinder, and in these cases one has to select what one does, what one shows, with great care.'

There was a rare and bloodless week of repose. The island had long been in a state of barely suppressed upheaval. The tale of the incident in the restaurant spread and fermented. Then things became so violent that Lionel took Tom with him every day to the office. The child heard his safety being discussed on the overseas telephone. He was to be put on a plane to England, his mother said to Lionel. His father shouted to Lionel that he wasn't going to speak to the jade but that Lionel must tell her that the father had legal custody. The jade said desperately, through Lionel, that he might have custody but that he didn't seem to know that it meant company. Tom listened, saying nothing. His shoulder-blades seethed with the pain of his sunburn as he sat under the old fans, which spun around on wounded wings like birds in a trap. In some five minutes between telephone calls, Lionel showed him a scholarly paper on the money-market that his father had written. 'London, the hub of the financial world,

19

the only place where a verbal agreement is trusted as binding,' said the frontispiece, under an engraving of a Wren church. There was much about trust in the pound. 'What's trust in the pound? Why does it keep the pound up?' asked Tom. 'It's the same as trust in God keeping God up,' said Lionel. 'Cashing a cheque isn't like having to go to church. I've had to learn the Nicene *and* the Apostles' Creed. Crikey!' 'You know that crikey comes from Christ?' said Lionel. *'Jesus,'* said Tom; 'Yes,' said Lionel, 'like pubs called "The Goat and Compasses" coming from "God encompasseth us".' 'People do get in a muddle,' said Tom. 'I like Harvest Festival and I like Christmas but I'm not particularly keen on Easter because of the nails. *God* gets people in a muddle, even more than trust in the pound. I mean, everyone tells you that ghosts are nothing to be scared of because they don't exist, and then they carry on about fear of a *Holy* Ghost. What's a virgin?'

'Someone who hasn't been in love, and so on.'

'That's what I suspected. That the Virgin Mary didn't like God much, let alone the Ghost.'

On the page after the frontispiece of Tom's father's paper on the money-market, there was a dedication in Gothic type: 'To my friends'.

'But my father hasn't got any friends. He's always moaning about it,' said Tom.

'He's got you, for instance.'

'Why didn't he say me in the book, then? And you?'

Lionel took stock. Then he said, 'Harshness often has to do with fantasies about sadness, which is sentimentality. Sentimentality isn't charity. I'm speaking privately, you understand. Your father often drives people away so as to test them. To see if they'll come back.'

'There's only one thing that's stopping him from coming back to us,' said Tom, looking at his father's treatise, 'and that's loot.'

He sat in a corner of the office while blacks in the street outside overturned cars and white people on polo ponies galloped into silent mobs of the blacks who were threatening their standard of living.

All week, there were telephone calls from Tom's father and mother, warring about his safety. 'Cant about peace of mind,' said Lionel in the office, giving Tom a dictionary for consolation to look up the word 'cant' and trying meanwhile to conduct a maniac exchange of currencies on Tom's father's behalf, although much mania was precluded by the fact that there was only one gentle and frightened operator manning the telephone system on the whole island. He got through once to a London operator: to a

West Indian who had been living in Brixton for nine years. They had a conversation about bus routes. The West Indian now had a Brixton accent.

'I swear I was never so tickled to hear a voice in my life,' said Lionel when the call was over.

'It's Friday,' said Tom.

'The day for your pocket money. I hadn't forgotten.'

Tom said steadily. 'No, the day for my father's allowance. Let me make out the cheque this time, not just sign it.'

Lionel considered the point. If Tom wanted to write to his father privately, he had the right, Lionel thought. People should be allowed to leap into their life, Lionel thought.

Tom went to the bank with the black girl who collected office orders for coffee and Coke. She was often forced to spend half of her wages on the orders because thirty-odd people would be in conference some days and would always neglect to pay her back for what she had bought them. Tom made out a cheque for ten thousand in the local currency. The girl was known at the bank, and he had his passport with him; his plan perhaps worked because of the crisis, perhaps because the cheque had the usual weekly signature, perhaps because the teller and the bank manager were also both black. Tom tried to give a thousand in notes to the girl, whose poverty he comprehended, but she refused the money and stood back, far off, watching him. Then he burnt his father's grievous money in a tin rubbish bin. A band of blacks collected around the flames and sang, not knowing what was burning until one of them detected a great many bank notes left among the cinders. 'Have them!' shouted Tom, wishing to be quickly rid of the stuff, and scared of the anger he knew to be on its way in the crowd. 'Have them! They're my father's and he can't use them because of the tax.' Some of the crowd, recognizing a high-born white child, thought he said 'taxi'. Few of them had heard of tax, because there was none on the island, though there were several taxis for white travellers. Several who understood him were devout men who thought that 'tax' was an evil word in the mouth of a child. Some of the crowd drifted away. Others merely watched. The rest fought over the money, angered by the white boy's arrogance in burning what they needed. The white patriarchs, hearing of the event, said he had been made wanton by the absence of a father. As though many people on the island so much as knew who their father was.

When Tom told Lionel what he had done, Lionel thought for a while and then found somewhere in the simmering town to sit outside on a bench with the boy.

'I've got you the sack by doing that, haven't I?' Tom said. 'And the soppy thing is, I did it to have my father with us, and now I don't even want to see him again. I've just realized. At this moment.' Having a precise mind, he looked at his watch. 'It doesn't matter, does it? I could write you a cheque every week.'

'Don't reduce an irreducible act.'

'I've got to make a list. It's in my mind.'

'I'll go and have an ice-cream.' Lionel left, looking back, as Tom wrote a list of words that were in some way – practically or verbally – consoling and key:

SECOND HAND ON WATCH
NEW JOB FOR LIONEL
TELESCOPE OR OTHER ASTRONOMICAL
INSTRUMENT
SEXTANT
SKEWBALD
LEARN HOW TO COOK
'FOR ALL THE SAINTS' (proper tune)
MAP OF NORTHUMBERLAND
VIVAT!

Phone-In

'Hi-de-hi. Rise and shine. And may God give you many, many happy years ahead,' said Mr Rossiter in the radio studio at 7.30 in the morning, 'Mr Big Director, put through our first caller. Who's the lucky one?'

'Linda, Granny's going to be on with Mr Rossiter. Eat up your eggs. Isn't this something?' said Mrs Slotkin with her ear to the phone.

'You're on the *air*, Granny. I'm sorry I don't know your name yet,' said Mr Rossiter.

'Turn up my radio, Linda. I want to be able to hear myself,' said Mrs Slotkin, speaking over him for excitement.

'I said you're on the air,' said Mr Rossiter.

'Oh! You scared my mouth off.'

'Are you hearing me? There's a lot of background noise.'

'There's a steel band outside.'

'Could you shut the window?'

'I'm sorry, I'm sorry.'

'Hon, I can't hear you. Are you all right?'

'Yes, I'm very good. I feel extra good this morning, talking with you. It's like I'm taking a course for a degree. I respect the way you treat people.'

'Is your radio tuned to this station? I can hear an echo.'

'I respect the way you tell people when they're wrong.'

'Never mind. What's your name, honey? What's your problem?'

'I'm Mrs Slotkin senior. My son and daughter-in-law passed away and I live with my granddaughter Linda Slotkin in a lovely mobile home and my problem is I'm lonely.'

'You'll have to turn the radio down, honey. I'm getting the echo of my own voice. I can't hear you because I'm speaking over you.'

'Linda, you heard what Mr Rossiter said. What are you wearing that dress for on a weekday?'

'It seemed a special day,' said Linda. 'Your phone-in day.'

'And what's your problem, again?' said Mr Rossiter.

'Isn't that a pity? I can't hear us on the radio now. All I can hear is our voices on the telephone. Mr Rossiter, I want to tell you what an appreciation I have of your deep sympathy for human beings. Can you hear me?'

'That's very nice of you. I like to do what I can. Is there a problem concerning your mobile home? Repairs? Leases?'

'No, I'm just lonely.'

'With your lovely granddaughter with you? Mr Big Director is waving at me to tell me we have just two minutes more for this call.'

'I'm not lovely,' said Linda, audibly to the audience. 'I've reached the gangly age and I talk through my nose. Granny, ask Mr Rossiter if I should have my adenoids out.'

'Linda, sweetie, you mustn't interrupt your grandmother,' said Mr Rossiter, 'but you just send me a photograph and your address and I'll send you the name of a doctor near you. Mrs Slotkin, tell me about your activities. Does your mobile home park offer you enough activities?'

'I never liked Canasta and I can't take to Bingo and I don't drink. I don't believe in vegetating so I proof-read the telephone directory. When I've finished my work I go for a drive in my late husband's car to deliver the proofs.'

'That's a full and adventuresome day, Mrs Slotkin. Your trouble is that you're too hard on yourself. I expect you sometimes take your neighbours in the mobile homes for joyrides, don't you? You're a sociable person?'

'They turn me down. I'm a loner, you might say.'

'Are you an experienced driver? I'll bet the scenery around you is something.'

'I've been driving for twenty years but people get testy with me because I never did learn to make a left, its being across the traffic.'

'How do you manage?'

'You can do it if you figure it out. I always had a head for planning. Right and right and right again, and keep going parallel with the left turn you had in mind as far as you want and then one block further, and then right and right again, and you're at your left turn. I also keep a sharp eye out for clover leaves, which are a great blessing to people who find left turns a trial.'

'Mr Big Director is making his final signal. I'll have to ask you to hang up in ten seconds.'

'I can't ever thank you for this.'

'You've a good life, Mrs Slotkin.'

'Oh, help,' said Linda. 'Oh, hell. A cockroach has just gone into the toaster. Mr Rossiter,' yelling, 'suppose it gets electrocuted?'

'Honey, if you have a bug problem in your mobile home you're entitled to help from the manager. God bless you both. And now come in, new caller, and a good morning to you.'

'My name's Mrs Wishhart, Mr Rossiter, and I just can't believe this. My husband and I live at Peaceful World which is a beautiful place with a golf course and recreation halls and we sold our house to buy this to retire to. Only there's one trouble I want to talk to you about.'

'And what's that?'

'You tell them, Mr Wishhart.'

'Mrs Wishhart has always been an exemplary cook, Mr Rossiter, and they won't allow her to cook in the cottage.'

'Why's that?'

'We have to clock in for meals at the community centre,' said Mr Wishhart. 'It's the only way they can tell if we're ambulatory. We're always ambulatory, one or the other of us, and one's enough to get the other along. If you don't appear in the meal hall for three days they put you in the hospital and that's the end. If one of us gets arthritis we just have to hope that it won't last for more than three days. We're very spry, you know.'

'I can tell from your voices that there's something else on your minds, can't you, listeners? Do you regret selling your house? May I ask your age?'

'Our combined ages are a hundred and sixty-three,' said Mr Wishhart. 'You've put your finger on it, Mr Rossiter. Mrs Wishhart often gets up in the morning in our cottage and goes to the place where the bedroom door of our old house used to be. That's how much she misses it. We lived there with our unmarried daughter, you see, and we decided we were likely to become a nuisance when she got engaged, so we sold the house and had to pay everything we had for this cottage and the services. And then our daughter's fiancé was killed, and the management here won't let anyone under sixty come and live with us.'

'And she's forty-one, do you see?' said Mrs Wishhart.

'I'd like to look at that agreement you signed, Mrs Wishhart. You give Mr Big Director the address when you're off the air and I'll study it and see if we can't get you out of this. It'll mean fighting, mind. You've got to face that you've taken the wrong step. For the best reasons, but that doesn't help you in law. But we'll think of something. And send me copies of your wills. You know, sometimes we're up against a wall and we have to decide whether strong measures aren't the most decent. Suing isn't pleasant but we might be able to get you more freedom than you have at the moment on the ground of humanitarianism.

Humanitarianism to your daughter, I'm thinking of.'

Mr Big Director slipped Mr Rossiter a note reading 'Pity about mentioning wills, but good about daughter,' and the red light on another call came in.

Mr Rossiter said, 'This is a call from another mobile home. The Fleischer home. Now, I want you all to understand that buying a mobile home isn't just something for the retired to do. Three-quarters of the inhabitants are young married couples, or even unmarried. You'll find a sprinkling of young vegetarians. Remember your mobile van is never called a trailer if you're houseproud. You can get Hi-Rise two-storey mobile homes. Remember you're outside pollution, you're outside riot areas. you're outside high taxes. Mr and Mrs Fleischer, you said you wanted to tell listeners about your experience of mobile homes.'

'You first, dear,' said Mr Fleischer shyly.

'I've got to make the tea. I wish I could offer a cup to Mr Rossiter.'

'Well, we're in a world of pretend, aren't we?' said Mr Rossiter, laughing the strong laugh that got him through his shows. 'Pretending we know each other.'

'There's a wide variety of choices. You can get either a sunken bath tub or a flush bath tub, and the sunken costs no more. You can get a fireplace.'

'Fake,' said Mrs Fleischer.

'Not all of them,' said Mr Fleischer. 'I've seen a genuine WFB.'

'Wood-burning fireplace,' said Mr Rossiter. '*Really?*'

'What brought us to mobile homes is that we like moving around, hunting and fishing, etcetera. I kept thinking we couldn't afford to move around all the time, travel being the price it is, but I found we could. It's also a way of not bothering your kids too much. It gives us our independence. You've got to think ahead. You've got to remember that when you become old, young people don't look for your company. Not that we're getting near the dangerous age yet.'

'When I saw the mobile home I swear I was never so tickled in my life,' said Mrs Fleischer. 'We'd once been to a demonstration about them and it stuck in our minds. An exceptionally nicely dressed conjurer with two white rabbits in a show made gold coins appear like magic when he was talking about the savings of living in a mobile home, and the rabbits would disappear when he was talking about the use of space. Oh, it *is* nice, sitting down like this, the three of us together. It must be awful to be old and lose transportation, mustn't it? That's one of the blessings about a

26

mobile home. At first I was worried about their reputation. You hear a lot, of course.'

'Roughnecks?'

'People drunk as polluted fish, the rumour goes. Not an ounce of truth in it. We had a humdinger of a party when Mr Fleischer retired last year, and the office gave him $156 as a going away present, but there wasn't a sign of debauchery and everyone respected our new home. I was thinking, the funny thing is that you go away twice in life. Once when you marry, and once when you retire. And each time it's a ceremony to remember.'

'Splendiferous,' said Mr Rossiter. 'I can see Mr Big Director raising his eyebrows at me. The word just came to me. And what do you do when you're not hunting and fishing?'

'As and when we come to a stop, which won't be soon,' said Mr Fleischer, 'I've got the cement to build a nice entrance. I've got cement and rocks. I've had enough of lawn. Cement's more aesthetic.'

'That's not to say he's not a pratical man,' said Mrs Fleischer anxiously. 'For instance , he especially chose a conventional door instead of a sliding one, thinking of me with packages in twenty years' time. He was also against the extravagances that money can buy in a mobile home. Chartres ceilings, Roman tubs, wet bars.'

'A couple buying is entitled to talk back to the manager about things like that,' said Mr Rossiter. 'Listeners should look out for say, swing-door alterations that have been promised but not made. This couple we have the pleasure of talking to are getting the very best of the mobility of their mobile home. I don't have to tell them that there's a dreadful decline in resale value because there's no land attached, but I'm sure they've taken that into consideration and they're not going to want to move as they get older. Excuse me' – strong laugh – 'not going to want to change residence.'

'About hobbies, apart from moving about?' asked Mr Fleischer.

'We're going to be older, in time, you see,' said Mrs Fleischer.

'As long as they aren't against doctor's orders,' said Mr Rossiter, 'I suggest Air-ballooning, Axe-sharpening, Bicycling, Camping, Geology Trips, Glove-making, Harp-playing, Horseback riding, Horseshoes, Jousting, Juggling, Mountaineering, Picnics, and Yachting.'

Mr Big Director gave him a note reading 'Most of those are moving about.'

'What's Horseshoes?' said Mr Fleischer.

'Looking for horseshoes. Horseshoes are lucky, and the search can take you to all sorts of places. And then you deduce the description and life-story of the horse. The life-story *so far*, that is. It's not necessarily over. If contemporary, a horse's shoes are being changed all the time, of course. Then suppose you have a talent that your circle keeps exclaiming about – cooking, uncommon shawls, hand-made baby clothes – you may have the makings of a good small business. There's fudge. Truffles. Chocolate chip cookies. Mille-feuilles. Lampshades. Remember that failure to keep ledgers, slipshod delivery dates, overgenerous credit, tend to lead to doom. You could start a sewing shop, or a repair shop for the sports goods you like. Have professional cards made up. You could go in for cooking dietary meals, feeding goldfish: $1 a day is the standard rate for feeding goldfish. You could run a mobile library, though this requires capital, and a stable emotional state is an important factor due to the sustained detail work and the perpetual interruptions. You could consider raising night crawlers. Large earthworms that come out at night. I know a couple who made $80,000 raising and selling night crawlers for fish bait. You can get started for as little as $10 to $12 for 2,000 fine breeding night-crawler stock and in about four hours of darkness you can pack and ship about $9 worth of worms. Am I losing you? Worms are a fruitful small-business hobby that I've just been investigating.'

'You were talking about Geology Trips,' said Mr Fleischer. 'My impression is that mineral people love to mingle too much. What's your main advice about planning for the future, Mr Rossiter?'

'Keep the brain occupied and the physique seated.'

'I'll go mad.'

'There are ways and ways. I can see Mr Big Director waving at me to tell you about my hobby. It's marionette theatres. I build them from scratch.'

'A friend of ours, more sedentary than us, is doing that with a lot of his circle,' said Mrs Fleischer. 'Mr Fleischer does carpentry when the weather's bad.'

'I'd like to tackle some of the bigger things but I can never quite get caught up with what I'm doing,' said Mr Fleischer.

'They're putting on "Little Red Riding Hood" in hopes of the grandchildren,' said Mrs Fleischer. 'We've only got children as yet but I daresay the group we're talking about is quite right in principle. You can't expect young people to turn up if there's no entertainment. The rehearsals have bogged down because no one wants to be the wolf who pretends to be the grandmother.'

'Can I ask you something, Mr Rossiter?' said Mr Fleischer.

'Anything I can do. Of course.'

'Why aren't you on television? My wife and I have been listening to you for the last five years and we have ideas about what you look like but it would be an ease to know. We choose to keep our circle small and you've become one of the set, you see.'

Mr Rossiter laughed his strong laugh and said, 'Mr Big Director will send you a signed photograph of myself with my best regards if you'll leave your address. Stay young. Stay healthy. We'll be back with you after this message.'

Commercial break

Mr Rossiter, aged eighty-one, which was the reason he didn't go on television, looked up at Mr Big Director, his wife, aged eighty-two. She brought him a cup of coffee, moving the microphone away to kiss him on the mouth.

'I wish I didn't have to send out these photographs,' he said, looking at a pile of signed and doctored ones of himself aged fifty. 'Here I am, talking to people about fraudulent practices.'

'It's legitimate.'

'It got on my nerves today, calling you Mr Big Director. You went too high up on that gallery. I couldn't see you. You know I can't talk to people when I can't see you. Will you get me' – pause – 'I'll remember in a minute.'

Mrs Rossiter waited two minutes.

'It'll come back to me a second.'

She waited another while: ninety seconds.

Mr Rossiter said, 'Did you get it for me?'

'You never said what it was, darling.'

'I get like this when the programme's off the air.'

'You mustn't fret about the Mr Big Director business. It started as a joke and it should stay one.'

'It's anti Women's Lib.'

'Darling, I'm eighty-two. Women's Lib wouldn't thank you for me. I was a lot more than a flapper when we were campaigning for the flapper vote in 1928.'

'All that about hobbies!'

'Yes.'

'Not to mention creativity! Bertrand Russell, Casals, Richard Strauss, Picasso; I say their names for good cheer until I could walk out of the room at the idea of the people being in the house! But at least they didn't go in for hobbies. Who wants work that's made up to keep you busy? You're like a prisoner sewing mailbags.'

'I remember feeling like that when I was a child at school, soaking wicker to make trays nobody wanted.'

'Well, we won't make any wicker trays now, my dove, not for anyone. You're an eternal object lesson to me in this matter, I have to say. You've never had the time for invented work. It's a great question; keeping the brain interested. Sometimes one finds oneself thinking but knows one's not getting anywhere, however hard one works, that one's just shaving the points of needles.'

'I've been thinking about this business of violence,' said his wife. 'This violence on the news all the time. It's nothing to have in the house. I'm much gratified by this programme of yours, you know. The news is full of adversity. My experience is that violence is worst when you see it on television, next worst when you see it in a newspaper, and not really bad at all when it's happening to you.'

Programme

Mr Rossiter's first caller after the commercial break, Mr Anthony, said vehemently, 'Right now there are two hundred thousand young Communists in psychiatry. That's where the violence is coming from. They don't believe in the Almighty but they want to change people's beliefs. A person's mind isn't something to tamper with.'

Mrs Anthony said, 'Dear, Mr Rossiter may not agree. I don't believe I agree with you about change. Think of the first moonshot, dear. Mr Rossiter, we were all different after those first boys came down from the moon. I'll never forget seeing Neil's leg coming out of whatever it is: the module, was it? Like he was feeling for the bottom of the ocean and didn't know if he was in his depth or not.'

'And kids! Apart from psychiatry, and Communism, there's kids and drugs,' said Mr Anthony.

'We don't meet many kids, living here in a mobile home, Mr Rossiter. We don't meet the people in the other homes, either. You wonder what's in their minds. Of course, if they weren't here they could maybe see more of their kids, but that would depend on the kids, wouldn't it?'

'What's your question, Mr Anthony?'

'Well, I'll say it for him,' said Mrs Anthony. 'His father left all his savings to my husband's sister, thinking she hadn't got the earning power of the two of us. She tied it all up in a little house that's bequeathed to the Police Athletic League for use as a gym, and when she died my husband was forced to pay for her funeral because she hadn't left any money.'

Her husband broke in, crying, his voice high in pitch. 'And when I die, who's going to pay for *my* funeral? Let alone Mrs Anthony's, a woman's always being more expensive because of the flowers? What I want to know is, Mr Rossiter, can I sue the Police Athletic League?'

'You'd better send me a copy of the trusts and I'll put you on to a good lawyer, if you'll give your address to Mr Big Director.'

'And what'll *that* cost me, I'd like to know? In the United States of America?'

'Well, if you don't like it here, it's a free country,' said Mr Rossiter, distressed.

'Well, if it was a free country, he'd probably take a taxi free somewhere else,' said Mrs Anthony.

'Have you got some coffee there for him?' said Mr Rossiter. 'Are you sitting next to him?'

Commercial break

Mr Rossiter shook. Mrs Rossiter was standing beside him and had coffee with him.

'To talk about his wife's funeral being more expensive! To grumble about paying for his sister being buried! The stinginess we turn up in this programme!'

'Have you thought, dear, about getting a driver's licence? I think it's time. You can't depend on my always being here to drive us. Suppose I'm the first to go.'

He glared at her and roared, 'You *can't* be! There are some suggestions that go too far!'

They sat in silence while the commercial finished.

'What are we doing?' said Mr Rossiter. 'Doing this programme week after week? We're not exactly serving people who make events.'

'It's difficult to serve someone who makes events. One can best serve someone who is subject to them.'

Programme

Mr Tyler telephoned. 'Good morning, Mr Rossiter. There were several things I wanted to talk to you about.'

'Any help I can give.'

'You're an ear, you see, like my wife. For instance, our foreign policy. I never approved of the recent military graft.'

'Draft,' said Mrs Tyler.

31

'Oh, is it draft? Well, graft's no misnomer. We're a little bit old.'

'He's eighty-seven and I'm eighty-five,' said Mrs Tyler. 'Our average age is exactly half-way between us every November because we were each born in a November. We still work three hours a day each, but it's not enough for us.'

'People are lucky who work all the time,' said Mr Tyler. 'Teachers, writers. Carpenters and electricians get paid by the hour but the trick in that is that they don't work the whole hour. If you were to ask me what I miss most, I'd definitely say working all the time, and the only work that lasts all the time is brain-work, which unfortunately my wife and I aren't up to any longer, apart from reading. The little luxuries you don't miss when you're on a pension, but the lack of interest you do.'

'Go on,' said Mr Rossiter, alert.

'My wife's a real old dictionary. She does the crossword every day. She says it's not as hard as it used to be.'

'I developed the knack when I was ill,' said Mrs Tyler.

'She doesn't take proper care of herself, Mr Rossiter.'

'You can't worry every time you sneeze,' said Mrs Tyler.

'How do you manage on your pensions?' said Mr Rossiter. 'Send me details of them, and your insurance plans, and your outgoings. Give your address to Mr Big Director. We might be able to think of some extras that could come your way.'

'One can cut back, you see,' said Mr Tyler. 'I used to smoke the cigarettes in advertisements but now that the taxes have gone up I roll my own.'

'We've had some wonderful pot-lucks,' said Mrs Tyler, laughing. 'For instance, we won a raffle, long ago, and two other couples drove us across the country in the fancy cars we had then. Oh, that was fun! Every evening, if we'd driven our ration, we'd get out beside the cars and throw something in the air. In the men's case it was silver dollars. In the wives' case, not having any, it was our shoes. Some of the roads were so ruckety, and made worse by cars getting stuck with the wheels racing, that we used to drive across the sun-baked meadows and prairies out of kindness to our country's lovely automobiles, and because we had never before had the pleasure of seeing the continent at full stretch. Well, we had a lot of gaiety going, and we were all fools, and we're still alive.'

'You've lost your health again since yesterday,' said Mr Tyler, his voice fading as he presumably put down the receiver and went into another room to look at his wife.

'I'll tell you a story about where we live, Mr Rossiter, as you've been kind enough to ask for our address. Well, outside our front door there's one of these old-fashioned mail chutes. It has a notice on it. I copied it down; I'll read it to you:

'NOTICE.
Discontinuance of Mail Chute Service.
The Management of these premises having notified the
undersigned of its intention
to discontinue the rental of this mail
chute, notice is hereby given that the
service of this chute will be discontinued
on or about
February 1, 1951,
and thereafter the chute will be removed from the premises.
Signed, for Euphrates Mail Chute, Inc.'

'Well, you see,' said Mrs Tyler, 'now it's nearly twenty-five years later, and the chute's still here, and I'm still here.'

The Sports Chemist

I was brought up in a house so silent, where communion ran so thin on the ground that no serious thought or crime could be calculated to erupt. No crime has yet occurred. My father is an untalkative surgeon with interests in linguistic philosophy. Vocally, his only moments of the rule of instinct are the ones when he yells at anybody for leaving a glass of sherry beside a chair on the carpet. My mother has spent forty years studying the four years between 1488 and 1492 in England and Europe, laterally. I became a research chemist: a poor one, I think.

'You're weedy, Ned,' my mother said to me when I was eight.

'Mr Kynaston,' my mother said to my tutor the same day, 'Ned's weedy.'

'I know,' I said.

'I know,' said Mr Kynaston.

'Malt?' said my mother.

'No,' said Mr Kynaston, who was my friend. He usually bowed to my mother, fearing for his job, but not in this encounter. Heroism lies in not being as weak as at other times, perhaps.

'You're like a wraith,' my beautiful girl said to me forty years later. Her name was Poll. Her eyes as she said it were soft for the first time, though I had loved her for ages. 'You don't get enough exercise.'

'I don't get any exercise at all, do I? Apart from walking upstairs to the lab,' I said, 'and pushing your car when it won't start.'

'You're too thin. You'd develop weight if you developed muscle, wouldn't you? You've always told me you do.'

'Four pounds in February every year when we used to go skiing. And I got huge in the army in Belgium.'

'Huge? You don't look huge in the photographs.'

'Huge for me, I mean.' I thought of the days of health when I used to stay up all night and dance at Cambridge May Balls. 'I once milked a cow at breakfast time when I had a boiled shirt and tails on. My eyes didn't even look bleary when I shaved after kedgeree for breakfast,' I said. Such a time is over, thank heaven.

'You're talking as if it's all finished,' said Poll. She looked gentle, and she put her hands round her face, I think not wishing to be importunate at that moment by doing it to mine.

'Well, you could certainly say I'm finished as a squash ace,' I said, feeling sure she would know I had never been much of an ace.

'I didn't even know you played squash,' she said.

She started to play squash with me, hoping I would develop muscle. Her hopes were all young and touching. It was six months before I noticed that she had been playing with her left hand so that I should have a chance of winning.

She agreed to live with me. I was, am, in devotion almost abject. I try to secrete the devotion beneath work, because it is obviously an embarrassment to her. She is one of the new. She inclines very little to the lyric. Away from it, rather. Perhaps this is because of her emphatic good health. Her well-being is stupendous and she appears almost to want to dispense it. 'Have some of this,' she seems to say, as though her stamina were a cake, while she goes around the flat doing backbends or throwing tennis balls so precisely up to the ceiling that the shadow of the fluff simply touches the paint without grazing it. I watch, feeling much in love with her. I don't believe she would approve of such romanticism. She is too brisk for that, at least in the daytime. At night, on the other hand, she will often wake abruptly after a recurring bad dream. I once said, 'What were you frightened of?'

'Of suffocating,' she said.

I took Poll to see my mother on Mamma's eightieth birthday. She was a beauty who lay now in bed wearing her pearls. At seventy-eight she had been put there because she had high blood pressure. At seventy-nine she had grown testy one night about being held captive in a single room of her great house. She had taken her sable bed rug and her black deed box into a nearby spare room, and on the way she had fallen and broken her hip. A pin had been put into the joint. A fortnight after coming back from hospital she had got out of the bed in the middle of the night and climbed up to the top of her wardrobe to get out a beautiful old purple Ascot hat freighted with flowers and African ostrich feathers dyed lilac. She dressed herself in it and in her dead husband's favourite chiffon dress. Again she fell, and had been scolded for it all next week by her maid as if she were a child, which is the way we treat the inert, however lofty and beloved. I held her in regard and thought there was gallantry about everything to do with her. She began to be what the rest of the family called impossible. The member who railed against her most was an uncle of mine whom she had supported since he was at Eton and had injured his eye in the summer holidays while he was cleaning a gun. I have never been sure – psychiatry doing what it does, seeping into everything – that he didn't half mean to disable himself, since he was clever but lazy. He went on to take a first at Oxford in Greats, in spite of the eye, and then did nothing but ride to hounds and live off my mother. He married a girl who bred Dartmoor ponies at a loss.

Deidre, Mamma's peerlessly foolish sister of sixty-odd, who went to a fad healer about the moral justification of prosperity and about the state of her sister's hip, would appear for lettuce sandwiches at my mother's house each week and bring a brace of pheasant or a bunch of grapes from the vineyard in her greenhouse.

Poll and I happened to be in Mamma's room one day when Aunt Deirdre was announced. She came in with the atmosphere of urgency that is so out of key to a hostess who has all day to spare in bed. 'I can only stay a minute,' Deirdre said. 'I've brought you some cream from the home farm. Who's this?' She nodded towards Poll.

'A friend of Ned's,' said my mother, who had always had a succinctness of spirit that forbade catechizing. I remember my father and various tutors running their heads into that particular wall. 'Poll, dear, this is my younger sister, Mrs Farquhar. Deirdre, this is Miss Clayton.'

'Where are the lettuce sandwiches?' Deirdre asked, looking as if she were already preparing to go.

'Decent lettuces are out of season. You can only get ones that taste like silver polish,' said Mamma. 'We could ask cook for honey, or watercress, or strawberry jam.'

'You should have let me know,' said Deirdre. 'I could have brought some iron rations up from the greenhouse.'

'What does she mean?' Poll whispered to me.

'Lettuces aren't iron rations, dear,' my mother said to Deirdre patiently. 'You're not up Everest. I've often lived for weeks on bread and marmalade. Lettuces could never be the last ditch.' She looked with esteem at a thriller she was reading that lay on her bedside table under her silver lorgnette. Under it there was the score of an early Beethoven quartet. She had always read scores as easily as other people read books. She seemed to prefer it to listening to the gramophone. I have seen an electroencephalograph specialist reading reels of brainwave recordings in the same way.

Deirdre suddenly started to cry.

'What is it?' my mother asked.

'Percy forgot my birthday.'

'Percy's her husband,' I said to Poll.

'When I pointed it out,' Deirdre said, sniffling, 'he only said rather irritably that he'd given me a nice little kiss the night before.'

'Deirdre, I forgot as well, but we're both too old to be troubled by such things, don't you agree?' my mother said firmly. 'You must be over sixty, and I'm dilapidated.'

'But limber,' Deirdre said, with surprising grace. 'You can do ballet.'

'Only on one leg now,' said my mother, 'I do practice every day with one.'

'You're much more athletic than Ned,' Poll said, interested.

'Ned works with his brain,' said my mother, though she was actually more brainy than anyone else in the room. 'My intellect is not up to much, except when it comes to the question of Cro-Magnon man, which is my hobby.'

'But it's a strain on the plantaris muscle, doing ballet positions on one leg,' Poll said. She did them, using the back of Mamma's chaise-longue as a barre, and then went into a daydreaming replica of the motions of mono-skiing. I thought how marvellous she looked, and then I pulled her down by the skirt because she didn't seem to be thinking.

'Mother's still more limber than any of us with her fingers,' I said. Mamma kept a dumb-piano keyboard at the bottom of the bed and played double-third scales for an hour every morning.

'Ned's going to be as strong as an oak,' Poll said.

Deirdre got up, implying hurry.

'He's going to go to gym,' Poll went on. She looked at my legs, which always unfortunately remind me of Malvolio's, and thought. 'Well, if not an oak, a willow.'

'I must leave,' said Deirdre. 'The motorcar's waiting. I can't get used to having traffic wardens in our square.' She looked out at the family square and the residents' garden in the middle, not seeming to notice that the Norland nurses of her youth in their long brown habits had given way to *au pair* girls with boyfriends who often rocked the prams for them and played with the children. 'One of the girl traffic wardens was looking sinister outside your *own house*.'

'The one with the pretty hair?' my mother asked.

'How do you know about her?' I asked my mother. 'Ballet practice with one leg is all right, I suppose, but you do that lying down, don't you?'

'Against the end of the bed, or using it as a barre.'

'But the doctors surely told you not to walk? How could you get to the window?'

'I hop,' said my mother. 'One leg is doing wonders.'

'Perhaps you could try getting some exercise for the other,' Poll said gently enough. She had no anticipation of incapacity and would never mean to be cruel.

'Where's my fur?' Deirdre asked. 'Oh, I know, I left it in the car.'

'I'd better race down for it before it gets swiped,' Poll said, already at the door. 'What sort of car? What sort of fur?'

'The chauffeur will look after it,' Deirdre said absently.

After tea, Poll said about Deirdre, 'She looked as if she couldn't lift a finger.' We were on a bus. Then she said, 'Or have it lifted for her.' I laughed, and Poll said, 'Was that funny?'

'I liked your mother,' she said. 'The traffic warden she meant *is* pretty. And I liked the thriller by her bed, and her attitude to the lettuces.'

My mother always had a strong feeling for the commonplace. So has Poll.

We saw Mamma again several times in the next few weeks. They got on well. Mamma kept pulling Poll onto the bed while she was speaking, as if she were a paperweight to hold down her thoughts. At other times, the room would be full of ambrosial old men and women. 'Talking to them is like trying to get a Zeppelin off the ground,' Poll said one day, after doing her best. 'It's like trying to launch one of the airships in the big World War.'

'Zeppelins were in the war before that,' I said.

We went back to our flat, where I have a rubber plant. I watered it. I could feel myself seeming, as had been remarked long ago, weedy. 'The rubber plant's grown,' I said.

'How can you tell?' Poll said, doing a backflip and looking succulent in jeans.

'Because it used to come up to my top mackintosh button and now it reaches over my head.'

'I really want parkland, not rubber plants,' she said.

'I'm sorry.'

'Neither of us can afford it, but you know what I mean. Licence.' She walked around the room and moved a table. 'I was also thinking about your hamstrings. I wish you'd put on a little weight.'

'People have been saying that to me all my life. When I was small they used to try to make me eat porridge. I hated it, but the nurse said people wanted it who were starving in South America, so she sat me in front of it while it got cold and made me eat it up. I didn't believe her, not even then. Mexicans wouldn't look at cold porridge. I realized that when I travelled. It takes you a long time to understand the whoppers that people tell you. It's taken me all my life so far.'

'You're only forty-eight,' Poll said.

'That's old to start recognizing whoppers.'

'It seems to me you recognized them in the nursery. What did you do with the porridge?'

'I waited till Nurse was away from the room and then I poured it out of the window.'

'Every morning? Didn't it melt in the sun?'

'It was a winter when I was doing it. The porridge turned into a stalactite. I hadn't thought of summer coming, and cornflakes, which are even worse.'

'Hay food. Quite nice.'

'For horses.'

'What happened?'

'We were having tea on the lawn in June with a houseparty, and my mother was wearing one of her floppy hats, and she saw the pillar of porridge, and noticed me seeing it, and didn't say a word. Never.'

'But I still think you should try cornflakes again. You have the most peculiar breakfast. Cold water and black coffee.'

'It's the best coffee.'

'And sometimes cherry jam with a teaspoon.'

'Beautiful dark coffee beans.'

'I don't know why you bother with grinding coffee. There's just as much nourishment in instant,' Poll said.

An example of one of the difficulties in communication is seeing that there are differences in food between the nourishing and the appetizing, depending on age, place of birth, income, and so on. Probably income, mostly. There was a time in my life when I was very badly off for a classically educated English white, and when I lived on things that the hospital cafeteria served out of the dustbin canisters of, say, chili con carne that you meet in institutions. Those were the days when I was working most of the night, on calls as a resident of a hospital at any hour of the twenty-four. Maybe it was then that Poll decided to build me up. She made plans to take me skiing in Scotland. I have a very small convertible that we were to ship by train from London to Edinburgh. She asked me one night for a tape measure. My anklebones were already aching from trying on ski boots that day, and I wanted to lie down with her. I didn't feel up to the ski venture at all. I hadn't skied for years. But she said she knew I would love it again. My calves were hurting from the dry-ski classes that she encouraged me to go to every evening from the laboratory.

'What do you want a tape measure for, darling?' I said.

'And the car keys. How tall are you?'

'Six foot three in my passport. I lied. I'm six foot four.' She measured me with her eye.

'What are you doing?' I said.

'Measuring your skis in my head.'

'I thought we were going to hire them up there.'

'Yes, but their length will be in relation to your height. Have you got a broom that comes up to your armpits? We need to fit something else into the car.'

We hunted the broom cupboard. She expertly tied two brooms together. 'I want to see if they'll fit in the car between the seats,' she said. She lowered her voice. 'I don't mean to frighten you. But with my skis there, driving may be difficult with these. These are the same height as your crutches will be. I always take a pair of crutches for people in case of emergency. Your crutches are shorter than your skies will be when we're going to the lifts, because crutches only reach to the armpits, of course, as I said, but they're bulkier than skies. I don't know if they'll go in the car easily with my skis.'

Next day she bought me some crutches. She went to a medical outfitter for them.

'They fit perfectly,' she said, watching me clamber about on them. 'Let me show you how. The thing is to halve your weight between your armpits and your hands, and let the right leg swing to help you. Supposing the right leg is the damaged one.' She cantered like a yearling robot around the room, looking ravishing. 'Of course, they're too tall for me,' she said. 'I'm not doing it properly. One gets the hang of it very fast. The question is whether the crutches at five foot eight and the skis at over seven feet are all going to go into the car in Scotland.'

'Plus *your* skis.'

'On the train going up they'll let me carry them with the ski poles in the guard's van, if not in the sleeper.'

'You can't carry skis and poles when I'm not carrying anything. Not to speak of ski boots. I'll carry them, at least.'

'I'm used to it. You be in charge of the maps. I've never understood maps.'

On the Motorail going up to Scotland, the car fitted out with my crutches loaded onto the train, her skis were left locked in our train bedroom. They had steel edges. Very fast. 'I hope I can hire steel-edged skis up there,' I said. I had to keep up with her.

(After a lapse the night before, I had mustered the decency to thank her for getting the crutches.)

'Don't you think it would be a bit ambitious on your first try for so long?' she said.

I behaved sulkily and like a child. 'I'm used to steel edges.'

She laughed, wrinkling her eyes like a sailor in the wind, and said, 'Up to you, darling. Aren't you clever, having a snazzy sports car that's big enough to take crutches?' In the rocking train sleeper next day we eyed her beautiful German skis standing in the corner and I had a poor moment of wondering who would be needing the crutches.

In the end we settled on driving back from Scotland, with the unused crutches between us. She went to sleep, her head on my shoulder, pink with exercise and health. After six hours' driving when my kneecaps had been trembling with fatigue for the last four, I drew over to the kerb and woke her up.

'I'm terribly sorry,' I said, 'but I think I've done something to the top of my thigh.'

'Darling, that'll be your hamstring. It must hurt like hell. You should have said.'

'It's not a hamstring. I'm just stiff. I'm not as fit as you, I'm afraid.'

'There's nothing you can tell me about being on the slopes and busting hamstrings. Show me what it's like to walk.'

I tried walking on the road, with headlights flashing at me from the other lane. She ran after me and felt my thigh. 'That's a hamstring, all right. Poor love. It's something that we've got the crutches. Have a brandy.' She provided a flask of brandy out of the pocket of her ski jacket and found a thermos of hot coffee in the car. 'There's no room to lie down in the back seat, but I'll put the rest of the coffee into the hot-water bottle. Heat helps hamstrings.'

'You've got a hot-*water* bottle?'

'I thought something like this might happen.' She settled me into the passenger seat with my hot-water bottle full of coffee under my thigh and a rug around my shoulders. I felt a hundred and eight. She kissed me before starting the car. 'Bloody painful, hamstrings,' she said. 'You were fatigued with skiing, and the driving finished it. It wouldn't have happened with an automatic shift. My fault. I'm so sorry. When you wake up, have some more brandy.'

'I hate being this burden.'

'I had hours of sleep. It might easily have happened to me.'

No, not to her. I put my head on her shoulder. The brandy worked, and I went to sleep. I dreamt of chemistry and porridge and trees on the lawn long ago. When I woke up she was pulling into a railway station.

'I've decided to ship the car the rest of the way with us, darling. I stopped for petrol, and there's an early morning train.'

'Why did you decide that?'

'I was getting fagged and there's no point in having two invalids.'

On the train, with me trying to manage the crutches and Poll wonderfully coping with everything, we had one of the immense breakfasts that seem to exist only on train journeys: bacon and eggs and sausages and toast and marmalade. Poll had porridge. I had half a grapefruit – the menu said '*demi*-grapefruit' – and felt weedier than ever, in the middle of wondering how to manoeuvre myself on crutches at work. A parched-looking young man at a corner table was talking hell for leather in a high voice to a robust-looking girlfriend in knee socks. He was twenty-two, perhaps. From his talk, he seemed to be a theology student. He had a dropped jaw and a rather eloquent, struggling expression.

'As I say,' he said in his stringy voice, 'it's not the order, it's the people in it. Did you see Sister Victoria's room? No? Well then, did you see Sister Rosie's room? You did? I'm glad of that. They're not all like hers, you know. Sister Rosie's was done up for her when she came home from hospital.'

My hamstring hurt rather, but bacon and eggs took my mind off it. I thought of people going into alien hospitals, far from swinging around on crutches somewhere as familiar as my own laboratory.

'I didn't know you could ski so well,' Poll said.

'Sister Gladys' room is just a bed and a little desk like a school desk,' the theology student said. 'She's a good nun. But Sister Rosie's a *fantastic* nun. We go round in a trio. Though since you've been coming up it'll be different. "It's going to change the trio," Sister Rosie said, "with her coming up." They'll all be praying for you, especially Sister Rosie. She always says about you, "I'll be praying for her." The place has changed over the last few years. It's only lately that we've been allowed recreation in the common-room. What's the verb of "recreation"? "Recreating in the common-room." I expect Jesus would understand that. And I'm quite sure Sister Rosie would. She has a wonderful sense of fun. You must see more of Sister Rosie next time you come up.'

Poll said, 'Tell them at the laboratory that you bust a hamstring skiing. It's a very brave thing to have done. Don't think it had anything to do with the driving. That was just an after-effect.'

From then on, I had moments of cussedness and did without the crutches. There was an interlude on the train between Leeds and London when the morning country looked so beautiful that it seemed nothing could not be surmounted. Poll went to sleep on my shoulder again.

'We are all subject to the ridiculous,' she said out of a doze, to my surprise, and certainly not meaning the theology student.

'Some more than others,' I said.

'Darling, a hamstring isn't funny,' she said, and I started to laugh.

'I don't think I've ever heard of breaking a hamstring because of driving before,' I said.

'Most commonly bust in athletes.'

'But I'm not an athlete. How is that you haven't bust one?'

'Maybe it's got to do with having very strong calf fibres. Because of swimming.'

She made me an annotated diagram of the muscles that she considered vital. ('Of course, you know all about this, but anyway,' she said. I didn't. She always forgets what sort of chemist I am. Mostly interested in potassium and plankton. I believe she thinks I'm a sports chemist.) She wrote down the name of a physiotherapist for me. She didn't notice that she was lying amiably on me, so that my painful leg had the luck to go to sleep. The pins and needles when it woke up were small snags, but nothing to complain about compared with various damages in the war. I didn't mention the pins and needles, because I cherished them on her account and I have this impulse to hide from her how much she is loved. She has fair hair cut short at the back, like a cap, with a front lock that swings over her right cheek. Sometimes she looks about seven; for instance, when she does underwater somersaults while she is swimming, and comes up shaking the hair out of her eyes.

In the early summer, Polly started getting me to go to a gym. A big man whom I fell to calling Jim, because that was the standing joke of the place and because he looked discouraged when I called him by his real name, which was Herbert, kept taking my measurements and telling me to build up my thoracic muscles.

'I don't want to be a tenor, Jim,' I said. 'I'm a research chemist. My thoracic muscles don't mean much to me.'

'Swimming will build them up, but you'll need them ready for the surfing.'

'Surfing? I don't like salt water in my eyes. Not really.'

'Miss Clayton said you'd be going surfing,' said a friendly muscle-builder.

'*She* thought you'd like it, so *I* did,' said Herbert.

People are to be hanged for thinking things together, I thought.

'We'll soon get you into shape,' said Herbert, not listening to my mind, not even to what I had actually said. Perhaps it is not surprising that so few people pay heed, considering how little of interest is uttered, though a tone of voice can often engage the mind profoundly when the words are not deep. Herbert, for instance, had a voice that I found consoling when my muscles were red-hot that day, and I think he knew I was burning alive and also mortified thereby, because he turned the fan in my direction. He taught me how to fall. Falling is not easy. I mean, falling itself is easy enough, all too, but falling in the right way is not.

Herbert's gym is downstairs in a little room with an upright piano. The Westminster Library is comfortingly near. There are generally twenty-four-hour calm vigils going on outside St Martin-in-the-Fields for some political reason. It was a very hot night. I was tired after being at hospital all day, and I had to go back later. Poll had come to the gym to watch me doing falls and pushups.

'It's important for him to know how to fall properly, because the surf where we're going in Cornwall is treacherous,' she said. 'One has to swim sideways across the undertow.'

There was a man doing pressups on the other side of the room, watching his face in the looking-glass each time as he rose like a dolphin. It didn't appear to cost him anything, the effort. I can't do a pressup at all. Like many of our species, research chemists often tend to seem inadequate animals for the given task, whatever the task may be, a fact that one never finds out until too late. I was thinking about this and taking note of the man's face in the looking-glass. Herbert's brother was playing something rhythmical on the upright piano. The pressups kept time. The man had triangular eyebrows. He seemed to be about fifty-five. But staggeringly strong.

'I'm glad you don't look like that,' Poll said in a low voice to me. I had just noticed her speaking to Herbert about the falls he had been teaching me on the mat; I had seen her lips moving. We generally catch more than other people think. Or less, depending on the strain of surrounding events. In this case, I could see her whispering to Herbert.

'Jim, I think you have to be careful he's not frightened of breaking his neck,' she muttered (I have a very long neck). 'It's like a stalk to him. It's where the sap runs.'

Of course, this is perfectly sound, physiologically speaking. I thought it was nice of her to speak up without knowing that I would lip-read. The piano thumped, and I went on looking at the man's devil eyebrows coming up rhythmically from the mat. Poll gave me a bite of chicken sandwich. To stop me working, I think. Then she lay down on her side, put a leather strap round her ankle and pulled her left leg up and down against a weight. 'This is very good practice for doing the crawl over a long time,' she said.

'I haven't got much stamina,' I said. 'I can do a dead-man's float for hours, but I always used to give up half-way in races at school and then get whipped for it. Have you noticed that man's eyebrows?'

'They're like Satan's.'

'He looks as if he knows everything.'

'I think it's more because Satan's old that he knows everything than because he's satanic.' Poll sometimes says startling things. I had a wish to hug her, but suppressed it in the circumstances. Now the man with the devil eyebrows was curling himself up backward and stretching out on parallel bars upside down, watching himself all the time in the looking-glass.

'He's been here for hours,' I whispered.

Herbert was watching the man's muscles and making approving noises.

'How often do you come here?' I said to Satan, trying to be matey, though this is not something I am good at with strangers.

'Every evening,' he said. I wondered if routine were the key to something I hadn't hit on. There is hardly anything I do every day except take bus rides and plug on at research and go to sleep.

'What's your job in life?' Satan asked, hanging upside down on the bars and stretching a muscular leg out.

'I'm a chemical boffin in a laboratory,' I said.

'What?'

'He's a research chemist,' Poll said.

'What muscles do you think I'm weakest in?' Satan asked.

'It depends what you want to do,' Poll said. I wondered about that.

'If you were me,' he said, looking like Mr World, which I don't.

'Well, it depends if you're keen on gardening, say. Or ping-pong.' I realized this was being rude to him and said, 'Or soccer, or polo,' to take the edge off.

'Fitness,' he said.

45

I thought he said 'fatness', and said, 'You're not fat, just strong. You're not the sort to have a heart attack, I mean.'

'He said "fitness",' Poll said, after laughing with her face so turned into the mat that her leg wouldn't work against the weight. The little room got hotter and hotter. I practised a few more falls and did some legwork for Poll's sake to improve the sorry way I do the crawl, and then went back to hospital and picked hairs out of my back wherever possible. The hairs were from the mat. Herbert's mat is like a hair shirt; not that I have ever worn a hair shirt, but one can imagine. I don't know if a hair shirt sheds bristles, in fact, or if it is merely uncomfortable. I have a suspicion that I might cheat if the head monk weren't looking and wear it with the comfortable side next to the skin. It seems a needless extra bane not to, considering the ones that are inflicted on us willy-nilly, but I am not a brave man. Poll knows this and doesn't seem to mind, though she clings to hopes of conversion.

That summer, Poll and I went to Cornwall. We had to put off our holiday by one day because Poll had undertaken to buy two looking-glasses for an edgy woman analyst in our building who is justly alarmed by going shopping and once said to us in the lift that she couldn't bear the lack of looking-glasses outside the lift, because you could never tell who was standing behind you. This struck me as being rather neurotic for a psycho-analyst, and I may have maintained a brusque silence. At least, I tried to. Poll was more forthcoming and offered to go to Harrods.

'We're going to Cornwall,' I said, trying not to weaken and imagining a day alone with my flippers in London while she was shopping.

'It'll only take me an hour,' Poll said, who is at her best in any emergency she can cater for.

We arrived in Cornwall in the end by Aunt Deirdre's car, accompanied by Aunt Deirdre and a picnic hamper. I sat on the grey plush of the car with the picnic basket on my lap and thought of the grapes in her pretty vineyard. Aunt Deirdre had a fur coat on her lap, though it was flaming summer.

'Old bones feel the cold,' she said.

'You're not old,' said Poll.

'Well, I can still surf. I'm quite dab with my flippers.' She had flippers and a mask under her sable.

We went swimming the first morning. Aunt Deirdre said gaily that she was afraid there was no advantage in being thin at her age, because your skin hung like trousers on a circus elephant.

'You look splendid,' Poll said. 'So does Ned. He's been

wearing his flippers around the flat to get used to them.' She plunged into the surf, head under a wave, after gauging the undertow.

Deirdre followed. I went after her and suddenly saw that she was in trouble, choking for breath and breathing in seawater. Her head quite disappeared. Poll had her eyes on me and didn't notice. I called out to her and dived and tried to remember about life-saving. Poll suddenly took in what was happening. But she lost her nerve, rescuing an elderly common-law aunt not being one of the hazards she had prepared for, and she too went under. So I had two of them to try to pull back to the beach against the undertow. I remembered about swimming at a right angle to the beach. It soon became pleasant.

'Knock me out if you want to,' Aunt Deirdre said. 'I feel quite intoxicated. I'm afraid I might struggle.'

In the end it was Poll who started struggling, and Aunt Deirdre who mustered the resolve to knock her out with a small blow in the right place on the back of her neck.

'I'll support her,' she said, swimming on her back, 'and you support me.'

'Is she all right?' I said. Poll looked more beautiful than I had ever seen her, with her pale hair full of bubbles from the surf. I tried craning up over Aunt Deirdre to check whether Poll had any colour in her cheeks, but surf is no place to crane.

'Are *you* all right?' I said to Aunt Deirdre.

'Splendid now, thanks,' said Aunt Deirdre. 'She's much lighter than a sable coat. You think I'm empty-headed, don't you? Your mother always did.'

'No, I don't,' I said.

I saw that Poll had come to. 'Don't open your mouth,' I said. 'Breathe through your nose.' When we got to the shore, she lay on the beach and Aunt Deirdre gave her artificial respiration to help her breathing, which was faint and choked.

'There's some tea in the hamper,' Aunt Deirdre said. 'Hot sweet tea is first-rate for shock. She's shivering.'

'We'll rub her and then cover what we can of her with sand,' I said.

'Abundant solutions,' said Aunt Deirdre, my twig of an aunt in her pink-petalled bathing cap, taking a swallow of tea.

'You're a very strong family,' whispered Poll.

Catering

'With the divorce-rate you'd think it'd die out, but no,' said Angelica, the daughter of Mrs Pope the wedding caterer. She spoke to her father, sounding taxed. The smell of roasting turkey rose through the Popes' small Putney house like the smell of bonfires seeping through things. Angelica's boyfriend liked it. He would nibble her hair and taste gravy. Angelica thought the place stank. The weddings Mrs Pope catered were always on Saturdays. One turkey was cooked on Thursday night, the other on Friday at dawn, because the oven wouldn't hold two at a time. It was a ritual. This was a Thursday.

'Your mother and I can carve two turkeys and feed a hundred and twenty people with white meat only,' said Al Pope.

'Breast,' said Angelica.

Mr Pope was a thin man with a collarbone like a wire coathanger. He was one of those people who are tolerated or even held in affection for being a good chap and always staying to pay for the last round of drinks at the end of an evening. He was an engineer. He had gone to night school in the Depression. To get his learning he had trained himself to sleep only four hours in the twenty-four, with half an hour allowed for recreation. Now there were three hours an evening with the television. These were the palmy days, to his mind.

On Thursday evenings he could hear one bird loudly roasting in the oven. The other would be laid out, trussed and full of onion, on the table in the living-room beside his elbow ('taking my attention away from the set'). Any other day of the week he chose to watch television from a part of the room that could be closed off with frosted-glass doors, but he made Thursday viewing from the dinner table a point of principle. On Thursday the table was extended with two extra leaves, and it practically filled the room to the glass doors. The table also supported a hundred and twenty rolls of raw bacon, a vast bowl of fresh white breadcrumbs for the stuffing, tins of fruit and packets of jelly, bulk orders of cheese biscuits and ice-cream wafers and chocolate digestive biscuits.

'Aren't you enjoying your supper?' Mrs Pope said from the kitchen. 'You haven't come back for your seconds.'

'The provisions upset my concentration,' said Mr Pope.

'A steak-and-kidney pudding doesn't call for concentration,

48

dear,' Mrs Pope said. 'It's for enjoyment.'

'I mean my concentration on the telly,' said Mr Pope. 'You didn't take my meaning. It's nice steak-and-kidney.'

He heard his wife starting on the giblet stock. He recognized the symptons of the activity without turning his head. 'I don't know how you find the time on a Thursday,' he said. 'To make us a hot meal.'

'I should think she could do a steak-and-kidney pud in her sleep by now,' Angelica said.

'She doesn't do it in her sleep at all,' Mr Pope said. 'It's not always steak-and-kidney and you know it. It may be always the same turkey for her weddings, but it's always something different for the family. A steak-and-kidney's a lot of work.'

'Yes, when she's been on the go since nine in the morning seven days a week and up all night on Thursdays and getting a lousy ten quid for the whole caboodle,' Angelica said. 'What the catering comes down to is that she's being had.'

'It's ten pounds net, though,' said Mr Pope.

'Net is gossamer,' said his daughter.

'Net means no tax, the way she works it. Net is ten pounds clear. Ten pounds clear doesn't grow on trees.'

Angelica snorted, in a pretty way.

'Anyway,' her father said, 'she enjoys it, and don't go asking me why. You can ask her. It's her business.'

'She'll get clobbered one day by the tax people for evasion of the law,' Angelica said.

'You want to watch your tongue, my girl,' said Mr Pope.

'You're right there. You're not wrong,' Mrs Pope said to him from the kitchen. 'Do you need a glass of something, dear?' There was a pause. 'What do you want to drink?'

'Well, I haven't got very much choice, have I? Considering there's only the one thing I like,' Mr Pope said.

She brought him a pint of mild-and-bitter. Thursday was the only evening she ever found him trying. Her name was Ada and they were fond. She had a harmonious face with a merry aspect. A large woman. Their one child was Angelica, a name her mother had thought beautiful even before she found it was a kind of cake decoration. As Angelica grew older, Mrs Pope started to foster-mother small children for the local town council. Angelica, who called herself Andy after going to secretarial college, had grown up among a horde of farmed-out toddlers whose predicament had made them rampageous, demanding, or expectant of small fortune according to their natures, before being stamped with Mrs Pope's ample view of things and returned to other lives in due time. The departures took a toll of her. Or of Mr Pope, fiercely attached to the kids in the middle of calling them a bloody nuisance or too quiet to be right. To his wife's mind, he must have had enough of children and deserved a bit of peace. Anyway, she became a private-wedding caterer when Angelica left school.

'How does she manage it? Does she borrow a kitchen?' the headmaster of the secretarial college had said once to Angelica, who worshipped him and was in the habit of secreting what her mother did because she was determined to have another sort of life herself if it killed her. The headmaster had found out because his sister-in-law had used Mrs Pope for a function in his family and the name had made enough of a connection.

'She does it all at home, every cupcake and rock bun,' Angelica said bitterly.

'Must take a bit of organizing, all on her own.'

'She's got her girls. She's been using the same ones for years. She calls them girls but they're ancient. Three pounds each a time. One of them can't move about much so she stands there in the wedding hall and does the washing up. The others do the laying and the clearing.'

A wedding took the whole week to do it properly. Mrs Pope always rented the same small community hall. Sunday could be a day off, but if she had a wedding the day before she had to count the cutlery and the crockery to make sure nothing had been pinched, scrub out the tea urn, and carry everything out to the garden shed where she stored it in the week. In the early days she had hired the stuff but by now she had saved up enough to get her own and hire it out herself. Sunday was also the day when the napkins and tablecloths were washed. Ada had a spin dryer but it didn't get the linen better than damp. If it was a good drying day, she pegged the load up on the lines in the back garden. If it was raining the pile stayed in the kitchen.

Monday was the day for ironing, and for icing the wedding cake she had made the week before, and for what Mr Pope called the final conflab. The final conflab was with the couple and their parents, and he saw it as the day when future trouble raised its head in the form of arguing about which set of parents was to pay for any drinks at the table. The bride's parents paid for the food, the bridegroom's parents paid for the drinks at the bar in the hall (trestle tables, administered by Mr Pope, transformed into a flashing barman), but drinks at the table were often a stumbling block. Mrs Pope was also used to sniffing trouble. If there had been a bit of frostiness at the final conflab, she foresaw an edgy affair on the Saturday. She would call it a gannet wedding. ('I bet this is going to be a gannet wedding,' she had said this Monday.)

'We'll have wine at the table,' the bride's mother had said.

'Is wine at the table drink or food?' the bridegroom's mother had asked.

'What's the hassle?' the bridegroom had said, who knew some American to cover events like this.

'What your mother means is,' the bridegroom's father said, 'is that *our* wine or *their* wine? It's not food, you see, but it's not the bar, either. So who pays?'

'I will,' said the bridegroom, holding his girl's hand because she was appalled.

'That's always a good solution,' Mrs Pope said quickly. 'And would you like to have my cake stand or is there one of your own? Mine's only plated but it's quite nice, I think you'll find.'

'You can't afford it, not on your wages. Wine at the table,' the bridegroom's mother said.

'Belt up,' said the bridegroom.

'Your mother's only saying what needs to be said,' said the bridegroom's father.

'Well, if we don't have wine at the table, what are we going to toast them with?' said the bride's father, intervening with authority. 'That's a cost *I'll* assume. *If necessary.*'

Al Pope spoke up from the little part of the room that could be shut off with the folding doors to divide himself and the television from his wife when she was having her conflabs. 'Let the groom do it,' he said. 'It usually turns out to be the best.' He came into the other part of the room: their talk had brought to mind something he had been wanting. He helped himself to a mild-and-bitter after passing around a bottle of ruby port in order to soothe things.

'Happy wedding day, if and when it comes,' he said, toasting them lugubriously and then winking at his wife.

'I'll pay,' said the bridegroom's father. 'May as well go the whole hog.'

In the weekly order of things, a Tuesday and a Wednesday were the light days. Ada would check through the shopping lists and go to the cash-and-carry shop where they let her buy things wholesale. (She had a wholesaler's card, because her first do had been for a confectioner and he had let her borrow his card. It was for confectionery only, but he naturally broke the rules himself when he fancied a bottle of sherry, and the transgression passed into legality with the issue of Mrs Pope's card.) She handed on only the cost price of things to the client, and Angelica called her a nit for it. The dry goods would be stored in the hall, beside the foster children's old dolls' pram and tricycles, and Mr Pope's bike, and huge tins of biscuits and nuts and sweets, flour and dried fruit and stout and icing sugar for wedding cakes, and the parcel from a local printer holding a bulk order of matches engraved with gold and silver hearts and the couple's Christian names. The printer was an old mate of Mrs Pope's and did the job for her cheaply. The turkeys, the two looming birds, would sit around in the living-room to thaw out.

A Thursday was the longest day, controlled by the turkeys. While one was in the oven, Mrs Pope would mix the wedding cake for the next week, and then the rock buns, and then the flaky pastry for the fancies, and then the short-crust pastry for the sausage rolls. That was the night when Mr Pope had to have his supper on a tray.

'It's the one night he *has* to have it on a tray,' Mrs Pope had said once to Angelica. 'Why he always wants it at the table on a Thursday when he chooses a tray every other night of the week, Lord knows.'

'Inevitabe,' Angelica had said, doing the shorthand outline for the word in her head.

If Angelica came back early enough on a Thursday, she would be pressed by her father into helping her mother with rolling and filling and egging the pastry for the sausage rolls. They worked at the living-room table, using pastry brushes so old that they slanted like a rocking-horse mane, dipped into cupfuls of whisked eggs to glaze the pastry after it had been pleated at the edge with the back of a knife. Mrs Pope could crimp a foot and a half of succulent, buttery pastry in twenty seconds. Mr Pope would sometimes comes into the room to watch and to lick a spoonful of raw cake mixture.

'There was a chef at Lyons in Leicester Square who used to break two eggs at a time onto the griddle,' he said this Thursday. 'One in each hand on the edge of a cup and never an egg messed up. I used to watch him. He was behind a lovely clean piece of plate glass.'

Some other Thursday he had said to Angelica, 'You're not as fast as your mother yet, my girl.'

Patience came sullenly to Angelica; or perhaps only patience with her parents. She was a beautiful girl with raised eyebrows and poignant circles of pure white skin around her eyes. She thought her parents had a bad life. 'I don't want to live like this,' she had said back to Mr Pope that time.

So Mr Pope had put his finger into the raw rock-bun mixture to taste it, and said, 'What's the matter with it, then?'

'It's so cramped and you're both so old-fashioned. I can't even bring a boyfriend back on Thursday because of Mother sitting up all night down here.' Angelica slept upstairs in a tiny room and she was ashamed to have anyone there because of the creaks in the sagging single bed, not to speak of her unease about her parents' twenty-first birthday present to her, which was a reproduction Jacobean dressing table with mirror lights that Ada and Mr Pope had bought for her on hire purchase. If they'd only got out of Putney, she thought, there's plenty of nice modern stuff for half the price. (Her boyfriend Ron was in design.) It was enough to break your heart, but there was no telling them. Angelica took them to be conventional.

On Friday the finished fancies, iced and delicate, were stacked in crates in the hall, and the second turkey went on being basted, having been put into the oven by Mrs Pope in the middle of the night. She would also peel four hundred potatoes and finish preparing the stuffing and the green vegetables: one stuffing and two veg for an ordinary wedding, two stuffings and three veg if the family wanted it grand. Delicate little brussels sprouts floating in great pans, plates piled with chopped chestnuts and sage-and-onion mixtures, wooden boards of chopped parsley, crockery jars full of turkey dripping. Sometime after midday Mrs Pope would have her bath and then go to get her hair set for the Saturday; if she'd had the bath after the hairdo it would have spoiled the set. On Friday evenings she got the linen ready in the hall, and telephoned her friend the van driver to make sure everything was ready for taking her to the hall the next morning, and made a list of what she wanted from the garden shed. The turkeys were laid out for Mr Pope on the living-room table and he carved them. In the old days Mrs Pope had done it, but the time came when Al decided to take it over. He had a collection of beautiful old carving knives that he arranged in a neat row and sharpened in turn with a steel. Mrs Pope would relax so that she was ready for the do.

A Saturday was the pinnacle, obstreperous and exhausting. The van arrived at quarter to seven. There was the loading of all the crates to be done, and the hanging around for the bread to be delivered, and the picking up of the girls, and the chilly hall to be warmed by lighting the gas rings in the little kitchen off to the side of the left of the dais where the band would play. Then they set up the tables, and roasted the potatoes in the turkey dripping, and cooled the champagne if champagne was called for. Champagne meant a lot of extra work because of serving it at the last minute, but it made things festive.

'Something on your mind, love?' Mrs Pope said to Angelica this Thursday evening, slipping the rolled pastry over the long strips of sausage meat.

'No, why?'

'I thought there was something on your mind.'

Angelica went on basting a turkey with her back turned.

'Answer your mother,' Mr Pope said.

'All right. I'm fed up with not being able to bring Ron back. The place is so full of bloody poultry and fancy cakes you couldn't have a cat in. Ron'd go off his nut. Not to speak of nowhere to sleep.'

'It's a lovely smell, really,' said Mrs Pope.

'Not week in, week out.'

'Only two nights a week,' Mrs Pope said. 'And you get your changes. It's not turkey all day. Some of the time it's the fancies.'

'I've got to get a place of my own.'

'Who's Ron? Your current?'

'You've *met* him, Dad.'

'You can't get a place of your own, because you're not earning yet,' said Al, 'and that's that. We're not keeping you. Not keeping you from doing anything you want to do, I mean. Any other night of the week he can sleep on the couch in here, but not on Thursday. Not when your mother's up and down all night with the oven and might get a chance of a stretch-out.'

'Why can't I have your room? Why can't you sleep in here with her?'

'I can't sleep sitting up. Where'd I go? You can't have a working man sleeping under his own dining-room table. What's wrong with your own room? Many a time I've slept two to a single bed, and don't think I didn't creep up the stairs when I was a young 'un. What the eye doesn't see . . .'

'Mum wouldn't like it.'

'I don't mind, dear,' Mrs Pope said.

'Well, and there's the dressing table,' said Angelica.

'What about it?' Mr Pope said.

'Ron designs contemporary furniture, and it would upset him. Phoney Jacobean.'

'Your mother saved up for that,' said Mr Pope.

'Tastes change,' said Mrs Pope.

'Yours don't,' said Angelica. 'You're stuck in the mud. You want me to have the same life as you lot and I'm not going to, see? White weddings all the time. It's not modern.' Pause, looking for a fight, but none offered. 'I'm getting out.'

'We couldn't stop you, love,' said Mrs Pope.

However, something about the scene with Angelica bothered her so much that on Friday morning, when she had gone upstairs to put on a cardigan, she found herself sitting around with one arm into it and one out, and she had been there so long that she couldn't even recall whether she was in the act of dressing or going to bed.

At lunchtime, as she did every weekday, Mrs Pope cooked an extra main meal and covered it with tinfoil and took it down the road two stops on the bus to her old friend Willy, a widower in love with her. She had been doing the same thing for seventeen years. Willy would give her a glass of sherry, and she would sit with it to watch him eat for twenty minutes, and then come back again on the bus with the clean plate. He fancied different things to the Pope family and liked her cooking. He took to her experiments with pizza and spaghetti and French cassoulet, things her own family wouldn't have touched. Fifteen years ago she had had a child by him. Mr Pope hadn't wanted another. He knew about the daily visits but not about the enduring devotion. They hurt his pride, though not so much: not so long as his wife stayed. The two of them had talked about the child all those years ago, and he had taken her away to Morecambe to have it. Angelica had been left with a maiden aunt. Mrs Pope brought up the baby for a while as if it were one of the foster children, but after three years she felt the strain on Mr Pope and had it adopted by people far away. Willy had acknowledged the child and saw her quite often. Another daughter.

This Saturday, Ron had been spending the night with the Popes. Al had carved the turkeys and put away the knives and then lain down for the night on the table, which Ada had covered with two eiderdowns. He had said he preferred it, to get a jump on the Saturday; he held to his changed position with dignity, but it was so that Angelica and Ron could have the bigger bedroom. Mrs Pope slept on the sofa with her neck propped up on a rolled cushion and her head unsupported to keep the set in. Al twice noticed her lying awake in the night, and the second time he got off the table and went into the kitchen.

'You're not disturbing the fancies, dear?'

He came back with a mug of cocoa and said, 'Not when they're all wrapped up for tomorrow. My watch has stopped. What time is it? I've had this watch for thirty years and it hasn't done badly, but perhaps I need a new one.'

'The new ones don't last unless you go to Bond Street,' Mrs Pope said, meaning to go to Bond Street on Monday to get one with his name engraved on the back of it.

Dawn seemed to come slowly. Both of them slept in fits and starts. Ron appeared at six-thirty: a nice, dapper boy with a mouth as pink as a baby's, wearing jeans and a mod sweater, so that he could help with the day. Ada wore her best, under a white overall.

Angelica came down and made them all tea and toast, to give her mother a respite from food. The beautiful cakes and pastries lay on the bakers' trays in the kitchen and the hall. The van came. For the first time in her career, Ada failed to take in that the bread hadn't been delivered before they left.

Ron had come in his own car. 'I'll go back,' he said when they realized in the freezing hall.

'Don't leave,' Angelica said, to her mother's surprise.

'Somebody's got to,' said Ron.

'That's best,' said Ada, looking at Angelica. 'Then we can get on.'

'It's always the men who suffer,' Al said ritually. Nobody took much notice, not being meant to.

The women stood in the little kitchen unloading the trays of cakes and the crates of cutlery and the cardboard boxes of turkey wrapped in tinfoil. The gas rings were heating up the place; the people looked like coachmen on Christmas cards. Ada turned on the fluorescent lights in the hall and they started to set up the caterers' long tables. They wore white flat rubber-soled shoes, like nurses, and moved fast. Florence, the girl of sixty-five whose legs were bad, stood in the kitchen mashing hard-boiled eggs and cress for the children's sandwiches that were to be served at the buffet after the wedding breakfast.

'It's less children than usual,' she said to Ada. 'Is it going to be a nice wedding?'

'There was a bit of trouble over the drink.'

'I once met a girl who knew someone who'd got engaged at a place called the 400 Club. I always wanted to meet someone at a restaurant that was just a number. They're always the gayest.'

Al Pope was getting the bar ready. Ron helped.

'They've decided to have spirits, even,' Al said. 'We'll make them some wallbangers.'

'What are wallbangers?'

'You know, like people who bang on the wall when you're having a good time. If you're dealing with vodka you need something to kill the taste. A wallbanger is a vodka or a gin or whatever you please with orange juice. It's much the same as what they call an orange blossom, but the name of a wallbanger goes down better with the men when they're at a function. The vodka gives you a lift, you know. A lift, like people need.'

There was a lot to do. Spirits rose through the morning. Angelica undertook the cutlery. The band arrived at half past three. The place had warmed up by then and smelt delicately of turkey and roasting potatoes. Florence was basting the potatoes and washing lettuce and dicing cucumber and buttering bread for the buffet. The wedding breakfast was to be at fourish. The band had their instruments wrapped in transparent plastic, like frozen food. One of them was hungry, and Mrs Pope made him a bacon sandwich.

'The turkey is the bride's mother's, and though I daresay she wouldn't miss a slice – well, I'd rather have the bacon,' she said, worrying about Angelica.

'There's something up,' Al said in a low voice in the kitchen.

'I expect she's sickening for something,' Ada said. 'Perhaps she shouldn't be working?'

'She's got an easy life compared to what you had,' said Al. 'You'll find out what it is, I daresay.'

Al talked to Ron about the beer question. 'When you're being a barman in this situation,' he said, 'you have to watch the froth. Your barrels of beer are hot because of being moved, and you're apt to get half a glass of froth if you don't watch it. People at a wedding don't like that. They can turn naughty if you don't do it right.'

The guests came very promptly at four. There was anxiety and social effort. The band played. People slowly settled down at the tables with glasses of sherry. A lot of them had pushchairs beside them with babies sucking rusks or kicking under fluffy blankets appliquéd with rabbits. Full-scale prams had to be left at the door but pushchairs were allowed, though they made serving a nightmare. Ada and the girls rushed through the hall with the soup plates and then with the turkey, potatoes, and veg: four times round a hundred and twenty people, plus the obstacles of the pushchairs. Angelica by now was with her father and Ron at the bar, doing the table wines and rubbing the champagne glasses.

'Champagne's a pest,' she said. 'You have to serve the soup and clear, and then serve the main course, and then wait around while they eat their pudding and their cheese and biscuits, and then you have to belt around like hell to give them all a glass of champagne for the toast; and you *say*, "Don't drink this, it's for the toast," but they all drink it too early and you have to go round again. It's the pushchairs that are the the biggest bind. Mum's got about forty pushchairs tonight.'

'What's the trouble?' Al said to her while Ron was away with an empty barrel of beer.

'What do you mean?' Angelica said.

'Are you pregnant?' Al said. 'You could say.'

'No,' she said, rubbing up a trayful of champagne glasses fast with a glass-cloth. 'Ron and me's not serious. I want my freedom.'

Her father went into the kitchen to talk to Ada.

'I haven't got time now,' Ada said, flying about clearing the plated dishes of turkey and stuffing and bacon rolls.

'I think she's pregnant and Ron won't marry her.'

Ada brooded about it while she was working. She said, 'You'd better get back to the bar. Tell her I want some help in here.'

Angelica was tearing around the hall serving champagne. Her father saw that she was crying. The band was playing very loud rock. The guests, the older ones, were complaining to Angelica that they couldn't hear each other. The ones in love had left their food and were holding hands and wanting to dance. One of Angelica's false eyelashes had come loose, and at the same time as dealing with tears she was also dealing with eyelashes and champagne and pushchairs. Al sent one of Ada's girls over with a message that Ada needed her.

'Your father says he's worried about you,' Ada said in a soft voice, getting the plates ready for the buffet. 'You do the rest of the sardine sandwiches,' she said more loudly. Florence was washing up at speed, resting one poorly leg against the other.

'I work all week,' said Angelica, reasonably quiet. 'I'm fed up with having to do one of your bleeding weddings on a Saturday every time I can't manage to stay somewhere else over the weekend.'

'Weddings are what I do,' Ada said. Pause. 'I didn't know you stayed away on purpose.' A nail seemed to have been tapped in somewhere. Angelica looked irate and claustrophobic.

'Are you having a baby?' Ada said.

'Ron and me aren't serious, Mum.'

'That's what your father said you said.'

Angelica started to cry again.

'Get on with the sardines, you'll feel better.'

'I'm fine, Mum.'

'You think we'd be shocked but we wouldn't. You have it and I'll foster it. You've got your schooling to do and you couldn't look after it, I see that.'

'Don't be daft, Mum. I'm not pregnant now. I went to a doctor. I had an operation for it.'

'Oh dear,' Ada said. 'Oh dear.'

'It was an abortion,' Angelica said.

Ada stood there, feeling dreadful. 'You must be feeling dreadful,' she said.

'I'm all *right*, Mum. If you dare tell anyone I'll never speak to you again.'

'Your father probably knows.'

'I mean Ron.'

'You haven't *told* him?' Ada turned away to the gas ring and dealt with the tea urn, feeling as angry as she ever remembered. 'Well, I expect he knew really and didn't like to bring it up,' she said.

'He wouldn't have guessed it. He's not a noticer.'

'You can never tell for sure about what people cotton on to.'

'The thing is we're not interested in all that. He's got his designing and I've got a life to lead, haven't I? I told you, we're not serious.'

'How *could* you not tell him,' Ada said, laying out the plates. 'When we'd have looked after it.'

'You'd never. You're too conventional.'

'I looked after one of my own like that,' Ada said with difficulty. 'I had a baby like that, you know. But I thought I'd better give it away in the end.'

Angelica wasn't hearing properly. She was doing dishes of jellies and iced biscuits for the buffet. 'Well,' she said, 'that's what happens with fostering, Mum. That's why Dad wanted you to give it up, because he saw you getting upset when the kids left.'

She went out of the kitchen, grumbling about the heat to get herself away, and started again on the champagne.

'What was it?' Al said to Ada in the kitchen a few minutes later. Florence was there, trying not to listen, washing up faster than ever.

'She was having a baby and she went to a doctor. You know

what I mean. It wasn't her fault. She says Ron and her aren't serious.' Ada was piling mashed bananas onto bread and butter for the children.

Florence nearly dropped a plate but caught it efficiently and said, 'That was a close one. It's a different washing-up-powder. Slippery.'

'You'd better go out there again, hadn't you?' Ada said to Al. A woman guest came in and asked for some hot water to warm a baby's bottle, so Ada had to help Florence move the tea urn, which took up all three gas rings.

'It's getting near the speeches. You'd better get out there,' Ada said again.

Al wiped his forehead with a spotted handkerchief.

'I can hear they're into the cheese,' Ada said. 'Who's looking after the bar?'

'Ron.'

'He's a nice boy.'

'He doesn't like our dressing table.'

'Well, he's got a degree from an art college, hasn't he. It stands to reason.'

Al started to carry out a tray of cups. He looked back. 'That about the doctor would have upset you,' he said.

'I wish she hadn't done it.'

Al put down the tray, and she stopped thinking about the lost baby and watched his face. He was good to her.

'You could always have looked after it,' he said. The volume of the rock outside was terrific. 'She shouldn't have got rid of it.'

Two of the girls raced in with piles of dirty plates up their arms.

'Well, it's the modern thing, isn't it?' Ada said.

'It needn't have been difficult,' he said, thinking of Willy's child, whom they never spoke about.

'You wouldn't have been glad of another brat in the house,' Ada said.

'I wouldn't have minded.'

'No, you never did. That's something you say, isn't it? "I wouldn't have minded."'

Al went out to stand on a chair and start the toasts.

'Boys and girls,' he said to the guests, 'I am calling on you to get into the spirit of giving this young couple a happy day.' He was good at this, but today it came harder. The casualness. 'A happy day. Here on my left is your host, Mr Pickering. Look at his happy face. He is not gaining a son-in-law, he is losing a daughter.'

The best man had gone into the street ten minutes ago, feeling unwell, so Al did his job by reading the telegrams. There were rather few, so he read out all the cards too, and added an old chestnut of his own that always worked. 'I have here,' he said, 'a cable from a friend who seems to be in the fruit business. The message reads, "An apple a day keeps the doctor away, but what can a pear do at night?" He looked at the wedding couple and thought they seemed fairly all right, given the circumstances, and then at Angelica and Ron, still both racing about with champagne, and thought that they were more than a bit of all right, given a little good fortune. Ada was standing at the door of the kitchen so as to watch him, before she set up the narrow side tables for the buffet.

The girls and Ada and Al and Angelica cleared away the trestle tables. The guests sat around the edge of the room while they were doing it. One or two of the men made straight for the buffet tables unasked, but Ada stopped them. She always held it was right for the bride's mother to see first the spread that was laid out; after all, the bride's family was paying.

Florence was washing up as fast as before. Three buckets for the cutlery: one for the knives, one for the forks, one for the spoons. There was a beautiful box for the untouched remainders. They belonged to the bride's mother. Angelica and Ron were in there helping. Al was carrying a message from the bride's father to the band, asking for the conga. After a long wait, the band struck up: piano, drums, two guitars (electric). The combination was small, but it achieved a resplendent racket. Some people grumbled, but other couples danced. There was the feeling that ahead were thousands of lives that might be lived.

Autumn of a Dormouse

'Energy and pride are the roots of the best things we do: I think that's right,' said Mrs Abbott loudly to herself one night, winding up her alarm clock and setting it for five in order to think, five a.m. being for her a long-tested good time for thinking. 'Without them, men and woman are barren and without mercy.' She poured herself another cup of tea from the brown English teapot she had brought from London long ago, and nodded off in a bed covered with travel brochures.

Mrs Abbot was seventy-four. Her widowed son, Grafton, shared with her the legal custody of her grandson, Alexander, but the child had actually been brought up by her since his mother's death when he was two and merely visited by his father. The old lady and the boy had an affinity. They made imaginary trips through tropical forests and to strange islands far away from any mainland. Footprints in the sand, fingermarks on the mind.

Then Grafton, a rich stockbroker, married an heiress called Edna. He decided in a loving but rather theoretical mood to commandeer the boy. He and Edna had come to Mrs Abbott at the beginning of the school term and taken Alexander away. The boy didn't want to leave his grandmother and the world of atlases, and he was miserably homesick at his new boarding school. It was the first time he had been away from what he thought of as home. He stuck it out for a term and even for a vacation spent at school. Grafton had thought it the least disturbing way to cope with the boy's time off, because he was going to be in Germany on business. Edna took Alexander out to tea twice. His grandmother refrained from telephoning because she thought it might be disturbing. Privately she cried for the boy.

Eventually, when the interminable next term had begun, he had telephoned his grandmother at her Detroit home secretly from a telephone booth, calling collect, three hours before she had taken herself to bed to think.

'I hate this place. Can I come and live with you like before?' he had said. 'Why don't you call? Are you off me?'

'No, darling.'

'Then why?'

'Because I thought you were someone else's business.'

'Whose? Edna's been here. She's OK. I think boarding school stinks.'

'What are you eating?'

'A Babe Ruth.'

'Oh, good.'

'But why can't things be like they were?'

'Things never are.'

'Damn, I've finished the Babe Ruth,' the boy had said, kicking the telephone booth. 'I suppose you'll be like grown-ups and say this is costing you a lot.'

'The thing is, your father wants you with him, now that he's married again.'

'But I'm *not* with him. I'm in this place. Anyway, Daddy's always abroad. The only person I see here who I know even a bit is Edna. She took me out to tea, and the food was great, but I upset her by not liking the clockwork toy she gave me. I tried to explain that clockwork toys are for children and she got cross and said she had a *rag doll* for when father was away and I wasn't making the proper adjustment. She wants me to go to a psychiatrist.'

'I don't know about therapy for children,' said Mrs Abbot. 'We never had it in England when I was a girl.'

'That's what Edna said father expected you to say. He forbade me to write to you in vacation. He forbade me to telephone you any time at all.'

'Then where are you?'

'I escaped from a botany trip. I'm in a phone booth.'

'Why aren't you allowed to phone if *you* want to? I didn't want to break into things myself, as I said.'

'But I've got your letter. Edna said that father said he thought a telephone call would be disturbing. What's disturbing?'

'He meant getting in your way. He meant it might throw you off balance.'

'What's therapy?'

'A sort of doctoring. Therapy is for people with a lot of past, and by the time people have a lot of past my own hope would be that, given more experience, they would know enough to sort things out for themselves. Though some clever people don't agree.'

'I don't want to go back to that place. Could you ring father? Edna said that she thought he'd be back by now for two days.'

'I'll have a think about it.'

The old lady nodded over her tea tray all night. At five o'clock the alarm went off. The sun was coming up, in its usual way. Mrs Abbott got up with it, in her usual way. She dressed in sporting red, made the bed, and went downstairs to the atlas. At eight o'clock, when she had carried thought to a conclusion, she rang Edna.

'I'm still asleep. Who's that?' said Edna anxiously.

'Alexander's grandmother. I don't think he wants to go back to his school. He says he hasn't seen anyone he knows apart from you. It's been good of you to go.'

Edna whispered, 'Could I call you back? Grafton's still asleep and he might want to be on the extension when we're talking.' (More loudly.) 'Even the *birds* are hardly up.'

Birds. Flight. To keep things in the air: that was the thing. Small Edna, intimidated, spending her time with a rag doll.

Edna rang back at nine o'clock and said loudly, for the obvious benefit of a listening Grafton, 'We think Alexander belongs with his father and stepmother, even if Grafton's away on . . . Alexander would get fond of me.'

'I could fetch him from the new school. He said to me in a letter that it's like a swanky prison. I could look after him again willingly,' said Mrs Abbott.

'His brain would turn to mould if he went back to live with you. Forgive me. With an old lady, though,' said Edna.

'But he was so happy, and now he seems so troubled.'

'When?' said Edna.

'He rang me last night.'

'Your imaginary trips up the Amazon. Though he *is* crazy about them.'

'I have a plan for him. I promise you and his father that it will work. I've got it all thought out. Something more interesting and educational than joshing in changing-rooms.'

Grafton finally spoke. 'Hello, mother. You're not the right company for a young boy.'

'It's as well that you declared yourself to be on the extension at last,' said Mrs Abbott to this man of affairs who was, she still couldn't forget, her loved child. 'It would be different about Alexander if the boy ever saw you.'

'Let it be, mother,' said Grafton. 'He needs other boys, and men schoolteachers. The constant companionship of a lady of seventy-three isn't appropriate for him now that he's growing up.'

'Seventy-four.'

'Mother, let it *be*, I said. Leave it to us. You're bigoted about therapy. You're being fuddy-duddy.' Grafton cut off the call.

'Or concerned,' said Edna. 'After all, she has looked after the boy a long time.'

Edna kissed her husband goodbye. He was going to Japan. He always made it clear that it would be 'A waste of your time to come with me. You'd be lonely.' She started to look at an atlas in melancholy, and tried laughing at herself, though anyone else would have considered her one of the most fortunate and beautiful brides in America.

The child rang his grandmother again the next night for fortitude. He was running away and coming tomorrow, he said. He had his knapsack packed.

After her think, the old lady had withdrawn $69,000-odd of savings in cash from her bank. It was money her son didn't know of. She had been keeping it for hospital bills, old-age home bills, or to leave to Alexander. At a Detroit travel office she had bought eighteen open return tickets to Rome from Kennedy. 'First Class,' she said. 'Mrs Abbott, initial E for Emma, and Mr Abbot, initial A for Alexander.'

'One passport as you're a married couple, or are you on separate ones?' said the girl in the travel office.

'Mr Abbot is ten.'

'That's a half fare, then.' (No humour, poor child, thought Mrs Abbott.)

'And one and a half one-way first-class connections for Mr Abbot and myself from Detroit to Kennedy.'

Alexander arrived, sobbing, with a knapsack. Mrs Abbot told him what they were going to do. 'Fly to New York, then take an evening flight to Rome, which arrives at breakfast time in Rome, though it's the middle of the night for us.'

'You're not serious,' said Alexander. 'Daddy would be furious if you took me abroad.'

'It's only abroad in a manner of speaking. Just to keep us both amused while they think about things for you. I don't think they've had a jolt yet. Grafton often needed a jolt when he was a little boy.'

'Granny, this would be more than a jolt.'

'I've sorted out the timetable. We'd catch our breath and take the lunchtime flight from Rome back to New York.'

'It would cost a lot of dough.'

'The lunchtime flight arrives at early suppertime in New York, except that if you hang on for a couple of hours you can have a terrific dinner on the plane when we do the turn-around to Rome again that evening. And so on, every day. Think of it! Rome!'

'We'd hardly have time to see it,' said the boy excitedly.

'We never do anyway, on our most successful trips. We can read on the journey. We're going first-class. Nothing but the best.'

The boy looked at a pile of travel books held by a book strap at the front door, beside other smaller things neatly stacked.

'Suppose father tried to stop us,' said the boy. 'He went on and on about wanting to have me now that he's married again.'

'Your father's away as usual. Japan. Then the Common Market countries. I thought of Japan, but the flight times don't fit. This works perfectly.' She planted her slim hands down firmly, as if they were paperweights to save a rare manuscript from flying away in the wind.

'Suppose Edna tried to stop us, then?'

'She's got no technical right. But do you want to ask her about coming with me?'

'Not much.'

'Don't be short with her, Alexander.'

'She's all right, but she doesn't give herself time to think.'

'Don't worry about Edna taking us away from each other, if that's what you've decided upon. She's got no legal rights. I'm your next of kin after your father. And as far as poor overtravelled Grafton's concerned, what we'll do is leave him a nice letter on the door here to save a stamp and the give-away of the postmark date. We'll just say something reassuring and permanent. "Dearest Grafton, Alexander is quite safe. He and I have gone to Rome. Returning to Kennedy tomorrow."'

'You're not doing wrong,' said Alexander. 'School is boring. I learn more with you. Edna's kind. In fact, I feel sorry for her, never seeing father. Though he's not very nice to her when he does see her: he sleeps, mostly, and talks on the telephone to Hong Kong.'

'Perhaps it's jet-lag.'

'Isn't that what we'll have? Jet-lag all the time?'

'We'll stay on New York time there and back. That's the great merit of daily flying. That, and the first-class service, and the fact that no one could say anything about non-consultation when we'll be in touch with your father or Edna in your own country every single day. We wouldn't actually have to go through immigration in Rome, even. Not every time, if we were tired.'

Alexander looked at her alarm clock, which was on the tea tray she had brought down to do the washing up, and noticed the time it had been set at.

'Could you have a nap?' he said. 'I'll guard the door.'

'We've got our plane to catch to New York. For between, I

have a plan for us, involving a boat. I won't say more . . . A short travelling surprise between flights; I can tell you that much. And I'm bringing some provisions. Chocolate for strength, biscuits, fruit, glucose tablets.'

'They eat glucose and chocolate when they're going up Everest.'

'We shall be flying very high ourselves. Did I tell you we weren't going economy? First-class! Think of it! It's the only way. Not that I ever have before, you understand. This is an adventure. I wish it could be the Nile or Tibet but I thought your father might be angry or worried with our not being able to get back in a day.'

'Why not Greece? I should have thought you'd want to go to Greece, being a classical place. My new school gave up classics long ago. We can take Spanish, or the Spanish guitar if we're dumb.' He paused, and said with bitter pride, 'I take Spanish.'

'I thought of Greece,' said his grandmother. 'In fact, I longed to show it to you as much as Rome, but we wouldn't like the present politics and the flights are very long. Rome is perfect. Did you know I spent my honeymoon there?'

'What happens when the money runs out, Granny?' said Alexander, looking at her carefully.

'We'll have to see. The right things flow from the right decisions, and this is a right decision, wouldn't you say?' He still looked concerned, so she played a game of chess with him until they could leave by the taxi she aristocratically ordered. The driver took a long time to come, scenting in her a thrifty nature, but she tipped him handsomely.

'Isn't it fine,' she said, putting her arms round Alexander's shoulders, 'travelling so light? You in your jeans, with a change of underthings and shirts. Me in my travelling suit, which adapts to any climate.'

'And your books,' said Alexander. 'And the provisions, and your spare clothes.' Someone long ago had called her a frank packer.

They took the plane to New York, and then a taxi to a park with a lake that offered electrically driven bumper boats. The chaos of children steering so as to bump into someone else's rubber fenders as hard as possible was controlled by a woman in naval uniform with a megaphone.

Mrs Abbott climbed into a boat. Alexander steered. Their boat was number fifteen.

'Number four, keep away from number six. He's younger than you are,' shouted the lady with the megaphone. 'Number thirty-six, this is your fifteenth trip! Come in this instant!' (Pause.) 'Do as I *say*, number thirty-six.' (Pause.) 'Number twenty-four, you'll pay for behaviour like that! I'm going to turn your electricity off.' Number twenty-four suddenly floated silently in the middle of the water, becalmed. The little boy in it dived desperately into the lake in his jeans and T-shirt, swam for the shore, and ran.

'An adventurous spirit,' said Mrs Abbot admiringly. 'Have you ever heard of Judy Holliday?'

'No,' said Alexander. 'I like the name.'

'You'd have liked her. She was very funny. She was an actress. She would have acted that lady perfectly. Isn't the naval uniform dashing? Though I don't think she was quite fair to number twenty-four.'

'He was a good diver. Can you still dive?'

'If I'm on my mettle.'

Alexander didn't know what a mettle was, but guessed it in context. He bought his grandmother another trip with his own pocket money and let her steer. She did it with panache. The woman with the megaphone looked nonplussed and made no comment on her skillfully taken risks.

The old lady and her grandson drove to Kennedy by taxi to check in. 'Only hand baggage,' said Mrs Abbot.

'Duty-free goods can be collected on the flight,' said the check-in-girl.

'We shan't be needing anything as we're travelling first-class. We don't smoke.'

'Mementoes? Perfume? Accessories?'

'We'll be back shortly. As to accessories, I don't suppose they have anything by Molyneux here, do they? Molyneux seems to be a forgotten name,' said Mrs Abbott.

'He's something to do with showbusiness, isn't he?'

'No. He made my wedding dress, but it was long ago. Never mind. Other people recall him. Memories for old details are probably limited to people with time, and you must be very busy. Do we need to book our return flight from Rome for tomorrow?'

The girl raised her eyebrows but punched a computer. 'A return trip straight away would be very tiring.'

'My grandson needs to be back. But you say it's not difficult to get on any flight we want.'

The airline official looked at her, having seen the wadge of tickets in her bag. 'Are you planning to take many flights? You realize you'll be subject to search of the person as well as of hand baggage?'

'Very wise. Is there somewhere we could rest until the flight is called? I saw you looking at my other tickets. You have to realize that I come from England and the English have always been great travellers. Lady Mary Wortley Montagu. Lady Hester Stanhope, Byron, Lawrence of Arabia, to speak of only four. Of course, they had to do it largely by camel and mule. But a 747 can be made to seem quite spirited if one tries. Unfortunately our schedule doesn't allow camels.'

'You asked for somewhere you could rest. You could go to our first-class lounge. Would you like a vehicle? A wheelchair?'

'We've just been on a bumper boat and we're used to getting about ourselves. But thank you.'

In the first-class lounge she had a lime-juice and Alexander had a Coca-Cola. Then she had a cup of black coffee. 'I don't want to miss the fun. Though we must get our sleep. We arrive in Rome at two in the morning by our watches. I think we should stay permanently on American time for your father's sake. It makes a link. I wonder if he does the same for Edna's sake in Japan? Rome will be buzzing and we don't want to be drowsy for that.'

On the aeroplane they had champagne and then caviare, smoked salmon and *foie gras*. Alexander liked the *foie gras*, especially the bread and butter.

'Don't fill yourself up. There'll be more to come,' said Mrs Abbott.

There was a choice of chicken à la Kiev or roast beef. Mrs Abbott told Alexander about the cathedrals of Kiev. Later on they watched a film so bad they took their headphones off. Alexander produced a bottle of asprin.

'I smuggled these through the search area,' he said. 'I swiped them at school for you because I know you don't sleep very well. I've got your chocolate. I prefer chocolate as a way of going to sleep. Counting sheep never works, but rationing the squares of chocolate does.'

Mrs Abbot put on a pair of dark glasses to rest. Her grandson was quietly impressed by her debonair ease as a traveller.

'Are you asleep?' she whispered, after a time.

'No.'

'Do you want a comic? I bought a supply.'

Alexander read himself nearly to sleep and then said, 'Tell me about learning Latin.'

'I'm wondering what would interest you. Not the ablative absolute, not *ut* with the subjunctive. There are some jokes in Latin, but they're not exactly funny jokes. For instance, "*lucus a non lucendo*". That means, "the sacred grove ('is so named' is understood: that's ellipsis) from its not shining".'

'I expect it's a pun. That would be why it doesn't make us laugh,' said Alexander sympathetically.

'Yes. *Lucus* means sacred grove. There's a lot about *lucus* in Virgil and Cicero. It also means light, which is the pun about it and the paradox. There isn't much to the remark nowadays on account of the sacred grove being out of date,' said Mrs Abbott.

'And Latin,' said Alexander.

Mrs Abbott lifted her dark glasses up onto her white hair.

'You look like a woman pilot in the old days. The aspirin haven't worked, have they? You must get some sleep,' Alexander said.

'I was thinking about people saying "no". It might interest you to know that there's no formal word in Latin for "No". Or "Yes", for that matter. You just construct the question with *num* or *nonne* in the right place, expecting the answer "Yes" or "No". The difficulty is the answer, but there are ways to do it. In fact, I think "Yes" and "No" come too easily in English.' She pulled her glasses over her eyes again. 'For instance, if I'd been able to construct my questions about our trips to your father expecting the answer "Yes" – if I'd been able to speak to him in any civilized circumstances instead of on an extension, that is – then I think we'd have been able to spend weeks in Rome together seeing all sorts of things. As it is, we'll imagine them.'

'Will you be sued for libel?'

'Libel is about something written.'

'But you're still taking a risk.'

'No. We're taking a trip. We're taking a step. Nothing legally wrong or morally unkind. Do you know what I mean? You listen very well. You must be a joy to teach.'

'But there's danger somewhere, I can tell. To you. At my age, I should be looking after you when Daddy's away.'

'Your grandfather, who knew you quite well though you can't remember him, is a great source of strength. We're having a spree. One should be allowed sprees. People will tell us we're eccentric when you get to know them, thank goodness.'

'Another aspirin wouldn't hurt you.' Alexander read the label on the bottle. 'It says two or three for an adult dose, and you're much more than an adult.' They slept.

In Rome they decided to stay in the transit area without going through immigration. 'Immigration's a waste of time,' said Mrs Abbott. 'This way we can have a nap before catching the plane back, and read my books about Rome.' She bought a few more travel books with pictures at a bookshop and said, 'I don't understand Italian apart from musical terms and lines from arias, but one can generally puzzle it out with the aid of French and Latin.'

'Don't they speak Latin even in small parts of Rome any longer? What a disappointment for you.'

'I managed at the newsagent. The young lady was very nice.'

'Tell me about your honeymoon here.'

'I brought some photographs with me. This is the Colosseum. Your grandfather took the picture. I had to stand absolutely still because the exposure was very slow.'

'You were pretty then, too,' Alexander said. He studied her now, lost in the way she laid her hands flat and hushed her voice when she was finding something exciting. 'I hadn't realized you were even pretty when grandfather knew you.'

'You're the first man who's said that to me for a long time.' She paused, shy. 'About Rome: let's see. It's built on seven hills. There's no need for you to remember the names.'

'What are they, though?'

'Palatine, Quirinal, Capitoline, Viminal, Esquiline, Celian, and I forgot the other. Oh, Aventine.'

'I expect you forgot because its name is more boring than the others.'

'Romulus traced the outline of Rome in 753 B.C. Romulus and Remus were twins and they were thrown into a river called the Tiber and abandoned.'

Alexander decided against saying, 'Like me,' but his grandmother could read his mind.

'Their future good fortune was quite like yours, because the Tiber dried up and they were looked after by a she-wolf, and the twin who founded Rome turned into a god.' She hugged the child, who so abandoned dignity that he curled up on the plastic airport sofa and went to sleep in her arms. She looked out of the window and thought of her husband, of her son, of Rome. When the child woke up she said, 'You've only had three hours' sleep but we can rest as we're flying back.'

In the plane, Alexander said, 'Did you sleep at all?'

'Now and again. I will in a minute.'

'Try now.'

'The trouble is, I'm hungry.'

More champagne, caviare, *foie gras* and smoked salmon. 'Could we both have bacon and eggs?' said Mrs Abbott. 'It's breakfast time for us.'

The airline purser, after some hubbub in the galley, offered two hamburgers. 'We carry these in case of smaller children,' he said cautiously, not wishing to offend Alexander. 'We can't manage bacon and eggs. Beverage? Bloody Mary, perhaps a virgin Mary for the young gentleman?'

'What's a virgin Mary?' said Alexander.

'In this case,' said Mrs Abbot, 'it's tomato juice and Worcestershire sauce. You haven't any tea?'

'We could make you some, I suppose. There'll be espresso coffee later,' said the purser.

'It would keep my grandmother awake,' said Alexander, craning across Mrs Abbott to look at things. 'Look, there's an island bang in the middle of that river. What a place to live!'

'The Tiber.'

In New York they did a quick turn around, pausing only long enough for Mrs Abbott to send a telegram to her son saying 'Alexander very well love mother', and caught the flight back to Rome. They were again offered magnificent wine, Beluga caviare and *foie gras*.

'We're hungry for it this time,' said Alexander.

The stewardess looked at Mrs Abbott and asked if they had been flying recently.

'Yes. This morning we came from Rome and they kindly offered us these things at breakfast time when we wanted bacon and eggs. I think we'll splurge again on headphones.'

The stewardess called the purser, who knelt beside Mrs Abbot and said, 'Don't forget you can order anything you like in first class provided you order it in advance. If we'd known you wanted bacon and eggs . . . Our film is *Mame*.'

'Oh, we've seen it. What a pity. About the food; champagne and Coca-Cola and caviare now is splendid. It was earlier in the day we wanted eggs and bacon.'

They both slept well through the film, and woke with enough appetite to tackle the breakfast croissants.

'I haven't told you about how my grandfather and I came to Italy,' said Mrs Abbott. 'We travelled by what was called "hard". Fourth class. Wooden seats. On the Simplon-Orient Express. We couldn't get over the excitement of it. At every frontier the wagon-restaurant that the well-off used would be unhitched, and luggage would be inspected, which took time. And then, at five one morning, we were over the Italian border, and people on the platform were shouting "Cappuccino", and we drank strong sweet milky coffee.'

'What's Rome like?'

'The sky's a beautiful strong blue. There's a lot of golden stone that looks as if the last of the sun has soaked the place, like a street left by strolling people at dusk. And a great deal of marble, and old walls, and high columns. Three of the columns belong to a temple to Castor and Pollux that was built two thousand five hundred years ago. Now we'll do some school work. I bought a book about mathematics so you can teach me about sets. When I was at university we did maths by a different system.'

Alexander groaned, and went to sleep. When he woke up they were over Rome and his grandmother was looking down at the Circus Maximus. 'It held twenty-five thousand people. Think of Domitian standing on the highest towers of his palace and looking at all the people he commanded. He wasn't a good ruler. And look at the aqueducts, see? Where it's green. That's the Roman Campagna. And do you see the triumphal arch? The Brecht theatre company in East Berlin had a beautiful plaster model of a Roman triumphal arch for *Coriolanus*. It swivels round on a revolve, and there's a stockade on the other side for the battle between Coriolanus and Aufidius. I saw the revolve. The company travels with it. *Coriolanus* is by Shakespeare.'

'Was that a real journey to Berlin?' said Alexander.

'Yes. Your grandfather liked the company very much. Do you know something? There's a temple down there that has the most ancient inscription in Rome. It was found in 1899. It's what they call a boustrophedon. One reads it first from left to right and then the next line from right to left. You used to make up notes that way when you could first write, as a trick for me to puzzle out. I was very impressed, though for some reason your father thought it was a sign you were unhinged when I showed him one. Remember "boustrophedon". Though it doesn't really matter what things are called. It's having the new ideas that counts.'

That day they washed some drip-dry things in the Rome cloakroom and went through immigration to hang them up in two lockers to be worn the next day. They took thirty-seven round trips altogether. When the money was getting low and Mrs Abbott was wondering where life could run to next, Edna and Grafton and an attorney were standing inside immigration in New York. Airline officials who had started by happily accepting the huge scale of ticket-buying had to begin to investigate to look responsible, and leaked the story so that there would be publicity for the airline. Newsmen and photographers jostled behind Grafton and Edna as Alexander and Mrs Abbot hugged the family.

'We tracked you down through the telegrams,' said Grafton.

'You didn't even use false names, which was foolish of you,' said the attorney.

'How long have you been back? You speak as if I didn't want you to find us,' said Mrs Abbott to Grafton.

'A week.'

'Poor Edna,' said Mrs Abbott. 'With you away, if she was worried.'

'I started a law suit against you in Luxembourg but I'll drop it now that you've brought Alexander back.'

'I never took him away. We were in New York every day.'

'What were you doing?' said an aged newsman.

'My grandmother likes travelling and so do I,' said Alexander.

'What made you come back every day? Very tiring for an old heart,' said a ruder cub reporter.

(Alexander had been asked that once, too, on their first rapid return. His wits about him, as usual, he had said: 'We forgot to lock a screen door back home and had to take care of it.')

Edna tried to hug Alexander and take him away. Alexander kicked and screamed. 'I want to stay with Granny. I want to be an airline pilot.'

'We'll meet next weekend?' said Mrs Abbott to Grafton, Edna and Alexander.

'I'll be in Brussels,' said Grafton.

'You'll be hearing from us,' said the attorney quietly to Mrs Abbott as the group led the hysterical boy away. Suddenly he skipped loose to run back to his grandmother. He gave her the locker key for Rome, where her clothes were drying, and the remains of his pocket money. And half a bar of chocolate; 'Instead of *foie gras*,' he said.

'I'll write to you from Rome at once,' said his grandmother. 'And then I'll take a breathing space, and then I'll be back.'

She had enough money left for an economy flight back to Rome, and a quiet hotel life there for a short time. Her son grew in admiration for her. Her address was the Hotel Inghilterra. Grafton remembered it was where she had spent her honeymoon. 'What I don't understand is the money you spent,' he said in a letter to her just as the cash was starting to run out, and her life with it, as old lives do. 'You usually economized so much.'

'Ah,' thought Mrs Abbott, 'but it was worth the try. He'll see the point later.'

Those of the hotel staff who had been there for fifty years remembered her as always having been a courtly woman. They were pleased at her deftness at learning Italian at her age.

However, as she had said to Alexander, it wasn't knowing the names of things that counted, it was having the ideas. In her last days, while she was standing in the Forum and wishing Alexander were there, whom she wrote to regularly, she was planning to get a visa for China.

Flight Fund

Farnley Hall, Farnley, Northumberland. Flight from one of the great houses of England? What need to flee?

Ah. There are moments in the greatest houses when, say, a rabbit hutch to escape to can be a considerable resource.

Downstairs, the celebrated hall. A marble floor, checked in rust-brown and white like a giant chess board. Twelve Chippendale chairs against the wall. (Not chairs for reading or conversation, one understands. Placed thirty feet away from one another. Chairs to be looked at by paying visitors to the great house. Marked 'Not to be used' by stiff white cards lettered in Gothic writing.) Many clocks, all telling exactly the same time: 9.35 in the morning, which is one of the harder times, like 4.55 in the afternoon, and 3.07 in the middle of the night. Twin staircases curling up to the next floor and to a dark, wide passage, uncarpeted, intermittently lit.

The Hon. Edward Douglass, aged sixty-two, younger son of the house – the Earldom having passed from his dead elder brother to his nephew, Tony – was carrying a pile of books along the passage, heading for a spot of light shining from the library at the end of it. Reading as he went, he looked up and paused to shout a greeting to Blades aged seventy-eight, the clock-winder of the house. Clock-winding in such a house is more taxing than it might seem. Blades wore, as usual, a green baize apron and a belt jangling with keys. He was winding a pair of grandfather clocks facing the heads of the double stairs. A Romney and a Titian hung between the clocks. Edward spoke cheerfully to Blades from quite a distance away. He had a carrying voice.

'With the cut-back on staff, I feared the estate manager might have cut back on you.'

'They're trying to put the boot-polishing into my province now,' said Blades, winding.

'I can see that boots would be a come-down from clocks.'

'Anyway, I haven't got the elbow grease for boots.'

'No.' Edward, drawing nearer, stopped to think. 'Cutting back on us all, Blades. You've noticed they've shut up my old room. It's too big for one, of course. It always was. But they've no need of a double spare room now. His lordship's trimming down on having people to stay.'

'Including you, Master Edward,' said Blades, which made them both remember being much younger.

'Yes,' said Edward. 'But one can manage on less as time goes on, don't you find?'

The Countess, Angie, came up the stairs in a new and very short tartan skirt. Not a kilt. A mistake in these whereabouts, she had realized at breakfast, from her husband's looks at her. But how to have known that in advance?

Edward looked at her. 'Morning, Angie, now that we can open our mouths. One never did get a chance to speak at breakfast in this house.'

'Tony likes silence first thing in the morning.'

'So did my father. I meant to ask you, as soon as we had a chance, that tartan's nothing to do with us, is it?'

'No. The shop girl told me which clan it was, but I've forgotten.'

Blades said, without turning round, 'I think it's Royal Stewart, my lady.'

'Don't you like the red?'

'Looks like something off a biscuit tin for export.'

Edward contemplated the matter of servants who had been a long time in the family.

'But very nice,' said Blades to Angie in the next instant.

'I daresay you've got Scottish blood of your own,' said Edward to Angie. 'Blood which would entitle you to your own tartan, quite apart from Tony's. Though who cares about blood these days?'

Angie sat on the top step of one of the staircases and leant her head against the banisters. 'No, I'm not Scottish,' she said. 'I'm also not the slightest bit Royal Stewart, though it's nice of you to try to get me out of things. You do that, don't you? I've noticed.' She lowered her voice and patted the stair beside her for Edward, nodding towards Blades. 'Have I made another bloomer?'

Edward sat down beside Angie, the pile of books next to him.

'He may be upset. He's been told to do the boots on top of a lifetime of clocks.'

Angie put her hands to her hair and pushed it up, starting to weep.

'Don't cry.'

'One man with nothing to do but wind clocks. This *place*.'

'There are a lot of clocks though. Two hundred and fourteen, I've heard.'

'You grew up here and you don't know how many?'

'I was only a younger son. Younger sons don't count.'

Angie put her hand on his. Edward looked down at it. 'Nice that we've all got Northumbrian blood,' he said. 'You coming from Newcastle.'

'Blood!' she shouted. 'Don't you start! I'm not a brood mare! I'm sick and tired of people going on about blood!' Angie was Tony's second wife. He already had an heir by his first wife, but he wanted a whole cricket team of sons, he said. 'I'm a failure about kilts, and I'm a failure about blood lines,' said Angie, on her feet.

Edward stayed sitting on the stairs with a copy of Virgil on the top of his pile of books. Blades went into one of the rooms off the passage and closed the door.

'When I said Northumbrian blood,' said Edward, looking up at Angie, 'I didn't mean blood in any breeding sense. I meant in the sense of lineage, don't you know. Not that it matters twopence-halfpenny.'

'I don't feel like the mistress of this place at all.' Pause.

Edward caught at her hand. 'You *transform* it.' He knocked over the Virgil. Angie picked it up and put it on his lap. 'Sorry,' he said.

'Why do you always say sorry? It's never you who makes the fuss.' She looked at him for a while. 'Struggling with all those books yourself when there's a full-time clock-winder getting huffy about cleaning shoes.'

'You'll be near tears again in a minute.'

'No, I won't.'

'Not many women come down to breakfast.'

'The women in my family *cook* it.'

'Yes. I meant in this house.'

'I didn't mean to jump down your throat.'

'No,' said Edward. 'Tony was down before you and he said his morning was going to be completely taken up with measuring. *Measuring*. Perhaps it's a surprise.'

'Who on earth invented kedgeree? It's there every morning of life now and there's no one to ask why.'

'Tony?'

'Not when he's reading the *Telegraph*.'

Edward listened.

'I don't mean I don't like kedgeree,' she said. 'I just wonder every morning where the hell it springs from.'

'I daresay our fondness for it comes from the days when England had countries that were hot. The word sounds as if it might be Hindustani.' He inspected the pile of books. 'No, I haven't got the etymology on me. But the Empire builders in the

78

tropics liked hot stodge at breakfast. And you have to give it to kedgeree that it's very well suited to the cold.'

'I've tried to put the heating up here, but I keep being told that the right temperature is 45 degrees for the corridors and 55 degrees for the living-rooms. I keep being told that Tony's other countess –'

'Amanda, darling.'

' – that Amanda didn't waste fuel.'

'She was a lot fatter than you. Fat keeps people warm.' Edward paused. Angie stayed quiet.

'It doesn't matter about not having a clan, you know,' Edward said, getting up and holding onto the banisters to make sure that he didn't drop the pile of books he was holding. But one fell. 'Could you give me a hand with that?'

He watched her as she bent down. A touch of forlornness. Angie put a nineteenth-century book about birds on the top of his pile and laid a hand on the cover to keep the Tower of Pisa steady. Edward didn't notice the tilt of the pile because he had his eyes fixed on her.

'I think you look splendid,' he said. 'Where's your room? The place is different every time I come back. I haven't sorted out the arrangements since Amanda and Tony split up. First sensible thing either of them ever did.'

'Tony once told me he liked my long legs.'

'When?'

'Rather a long time ago. Before we married.' Pause. Some search in the air. 'Has he ever said anything to you about me?'

As Blades came out of the room off the corridor and started winding a small Queen Anne clock on a costly escritoire without a chair, Edward said, 'Amanda's were certainly short. Very definitely short.'

Angie shook her hair violently over her face. 'I'm *not* going to improve the breeding line! Importing long legs!'

Blades spoke to the clock face. 'You should get out more.'

Edward put his hand on top of Angie's so that they were both steadying the pile of books. They got themselves to a chair in the corridor. It had a tasselled rope tied across the arms.

'Not a chair in this house you can sit on. They've all belonged to Marie Antoinette,' said Edward, putting down the pile of books and getting a boy scout penknife out of his pocket. He cut the rope. 'Come and perch on my knee.'

Angie looked at the dangling ends of the rope. What dispatch. 'I unknotted that rope once but I still hadn't got the nerve to sit down. Wouldn't the chair break with two of us in it?'

'We're both quite light. You because you're slim, and me because I'm just thin.'

Angie sat down beside Edward in the chair. He lifted her onto his knee. 'You take up very little space, don't you? You'd fit into a rabbit hutch,' he said. 'When I was a small boy and lonely here, I'd sometimes sit in a rabbit hutch in the vegetable garden for the smallness of it.' Pause. 'Also, I had a nice rabbit.'

'Do you always have a penknife on you?' Angie asked.

Blades said, with his back to them, 'Ever since I can remember.' He turned round to Edward. 'Her ladyship's bedroom is just ahead if you were wanting a lie down.'

'Getting onto one's legs is more the meat,' said Edward. Then he said to Angie, playing with her hair. 'I wonder if I can still do "This is the way the gentleman rides".' He tried. Successful. Angie grinned at him. He said 'Hmm,' and felt his legs in a spirit of criticism. 'The muscles in the calf aren't anything to write home about these days.' He looked at Blades, who was up a ladder. 'You seem very fit, I must say.' Pause. Edward settled Angie onto his knee comfortably again and said 'Would you like to hear a story? An IRA man in prison said to the governor, "Can I send my mother my toes for Christmas?"'

'Don't suppose there was anything against it in the regulations,' said Blades.

'No,' said Edward. 'Later the man said, "Can I send my mother my left leg for her birthday?"'

'I haven't heard this one,' said Blades.

'Next Christmas he said, "And can I send my mother my right leg for Christmas?" So the governor says, "Now I see what you're doing. You're trying to escape."'

'Flight,' said Angie.

'Of course, it's a very anti-English story, but we've had a poor three hundred years in Ireland,' said Edward.

'The stories you told me when you were a boy!' said Blades.

'When we were planning to go to Ireland! Shall we go somewhere now? Shall we have an adventure?'

Farnley came out of his room on the passage. A thin, intelligent boy of twelve who was Angie's stepson. Angie struggled off Edward's knee, though too late not to be seen.

'I thought one wasn't allowed to sit on that chair,' said Farnley.

Angie walked over to Farnley and said in a low voice, 'Any news?'

'The post hasn't come.'

'Sometimes people take a long time to read things. Even important things.'

'Well, they shouldn't.'

'No.'

Edward got up. Angie said to Farnley in a louder voice, fabricating small-talk, 'How's the holiday work?'

'Lousy,' said Farnley. He turned back to his room, exchanging a glance with Angie privately.

Edward, missing little, said to no one in particular, in a way that he had of addressing questions to himself in company, 'I wonder what made Donne say "No man is an island"? Not true, eh?'

'John Donne was an ass,' Farnley said, on the brink of the entrance to his room.

'The more likely fact is that *every* Englishman is an island,' said Edward. 'Coming from the country we do, it would be natural. Seagulls everywhere.' He said to Angie, 'Did he mean that no *woman*'s an island? Are the sexes different? Are you and I?'

'No.'

The sound of typing came from Farnley's room. Edward looked around him and said to Angie, 'I thought that was *Farnley*'s room. Is it your office now?'

'No, it's still Farnley's. He's doing holiday work.'

'He's skinny,' said Edward fondly. 'But he might make a cox. If he took up rowing.' Pause. 'I mean, if he liked rowing.'

Angie said in a low voice, 'He's actually taking a correspondence course in how to earn a living as a writer.'

'Who gave him the typewriter?'

'I did.' Pause. 'Christmas and birthday combined.'

'He trusts you, I can see that. He'd have told you in confidence about the writing. Hope he sticks to it. Waste of time, being a cox. Is he any good?'

'Yes.'

'Oh, I am having a nice time.' He moved ahead, burdened with books. 'Now I'm going to have a read. You go and brush your hair and I'll be in the library looking a few things up. I like to get my bearings.'

Angie smiled at him as he looked back at her, and then went into her nearby door off the passage. Tony was lying fully dressed on the bedspread of their four-poster bed. A noble-nosed young man with a double chin coming, and bat ears that he plastered back with Elastoplast at night, though Angie had often said that she liked them.

He held out his hand to her without looking, and moved to the middle of the bed with his eyes fixed on the wallpaper opposite.

'Come and lie beside me,' he said.

Angie hovered at the door. 'I'd roll onto you without the usual bolster, wouldn't I? Because of the dip in the mattress?'

Tony didn't answer.

'Shall we get a new mattress as a celebration? I mean, there's no need to have a mattress that goes back to the *Domesday Book* just because you do, is there?'

He still didn't answer. Concentration on the wallpaper opposite the bed continued. Angie made an effort to ignore dampening of the spirit. She lay on the bed and held onto the side of the four-poster to prevent rolling onto him. 'Or is it the springs?' she said, concocting cheer. 'Could we go to bed?'

'We're *in* bed,' said Tony.

Angie was silent. Her meaning sank in slowly.

Tony turned round and looked at her. 'Now? In the morning?'

Angie started to unbutton her Scottish shirt, and turned her back to him for help. 'I can't undo this button,' she said, ignorant that his eyes had wandered austerely back to the space of wall visible through the bottom columns of the bed.

'Keep your eye about four inches below that middle rose on the wallpaper,' said Tony, getting up and looking for something in his waistcoat pocket. 'There's a proper time for everything. I'm hanging the painting at the minute. *Preparing* to hang the painting. The Gainsborough.'

'Blast the Gainsborough!'

Tony glanced at her with dismissal, then took out a gold pen and readied himself to make a mark on the wall with it. 'The Gainsborough hasn't been in your family for two hundred years. Is this the place?'

'Perfect,' said Angie tersely, not looking, because she had rolled over and buried her head in her hands.

'I wanted to get it at the right height for when we're in bed. This would be the top of the frame.' Tony made the mark, and then went to an open window to look at his landscape. 'What a splendid day.'

'Yes.'

'Oh, lord, there's Hilda collecting homing pigeons again. I can't have a senile housemaid behaving like a bird protection society on my terrace.'

'She thinks the pigeons won't go home without her.'

'They just like stopping on this terrace. So do I. The mystery is what she does with them.'

'She keeps them in the old sewing-room upstairs with your grandmother's hats. She's worried they won't get back without help. She reads the addresses on their legs and puts them in shoe boxes and posts them from the station on her day off.'

'Did she tell you all that?'

'Yes.'

'She's been in the family for years, and *I'd* never heard.'

'It probably takes a newcomer to catch onto some things.'

'She must be bonkers.'

'One needs a way out.' Pause. 'Blades, now, minds about the boots suggestion.'

'He'll have to do as he's told.'

'I don't see why.'

Tony turned round from the window and came over to her. 'You're down in the mouth, aren't you? Shall we have a baby?'

'That's what I *thought* you meant when you were lying on the bed, but then you didn't seem to.' Pause. 'It's only this button I can't manage.'

'Not *now*. Some appropriate time. When we've got the Gainsborough hung. Wouldn't that be the occasion?'

'Does one need an occasion?' Her voice softened. 'Could we hang it now, ourselves?'

'Couldn't the whole *thing* wait?' Pause. 'What's the matter?'

'Everything's about waiting.' Angie cried, and recovered. 'Well, yes, of course it can wait.'

'What's the matter, I said?'

'I expect it's this life. I'm not where I belong.'

'Pull yourself together.' Tony walked back to the window with his hands in his pockets.

'Did you know Hilda's married to Blades?' Angie said. Tony spun round, looked at her, and walked out of the door quickly.

After a while she found Blades, and hung the Gainsborough herself with Blades handing her the nails. Then she made for the library. Looking for whom? Edward, certainly. And Tony might be there with him: might have heard the hammering, and even have been pleased.

Angie found Edward in the library alone, reading a heavy book standing up. A long, beautiful room with windows to the ground at both ends. Parkland outside. Old books, paperbacks, bound volumes of radical magazines going back to the nineteenth century, a shelf of jigsaw puzzles, a table that was set for chess, red leather sofas and high backed chairs. An old haven, much used, though not by Tony. Edward was standing next to the long windows for the sake of light. Soothed by his concentration, Angie sat on a low footstool to prowl through the bottom row of books she had never looked at. 'They're all on contract law,' she said. 'I wonder if Tony knows? He hardly ever comes in here. It makes him feel low, I expect. The darkness.'

Edward spoke to her in an excited voice, closing his book with a finger in his place but still standing by the light from the window. 'I know every shelf backwards. Nothing's moved since I was living here. I used the place for escape when I was a boy, you see. There'd be no one around except Blades dusting, and he was always company. I heard hammering just now. Was it him?'

'He was helping me put up a painting.'

'My father had the law books on all the lower shelves when I was a boy. He knew I came in here to get away from the governesses, so he bought forty-five yards of law books to put me off playing truant. If I'd been any good at games it would have made up for the governesses with him, but I wasn't. I couldn't read the Hardy or the Galsworthy until I was seven. But I got through *The Decline and Fall of the Roman Empire* when I was younger than that because it was near the bottom. Have you read it?' Gay. 'You'd like it. The cream ones. Eleven volumes. Between *Chitty on Contract* and *Admiralty and Divorce*.' He looked at her more closely after catching himself say 'divorce'. Though he couldn't detect any damage given, he went on in order to reassure. 'Admiralty and Divorce is a branch of the law.'

'Is that why you grew up to be a judge?' said Angie.

'Yes, I daresay. Also because I was interested. I only gave the law up because there were a lot of other books I wanted to read. And bird-watching. And racing my Arab stallion. He died. Everything dies. The next lot of books up, apart from Gibbon, are about the Bible. But I was an atheist, so I re-read the bottom rows.'

'An atheist at seven?'

'Are you and Tony happy?'

'At first. I suppose I didn't know I wouldn't fit in. Why are you standing up over there to read?'

'It's rather small print.' He opened his book again.

Angie got up and put her arm round his waist, looking at his book. 'No, it's the darkness,' she said. 'But isn't the reading lamp over the couch any good? I've never used it because I always read lying down by the window in the day, and Blades brings in candles if he hears me prowling about in the middle of the night. He always thinks electricity might fuse.'

'Don't you sleep well?'

'No, but nor does Blades.' She switched on the reading lamp and stared at the dim glow.

'It's only a twenty-five-watt bulb,' said Edward. 'It has been for years. My father was rather stingy and not much of a reader. I used to keep a hundred-watt bulb in my sock drawer and smuggle it through here in the evenings, but it blew, and I hadn't got the pocket money for another one. My father thought my mother doled out pocket money, you see, and my mother always forgot.' He came over to the sofa and sat down beside her. 'Does Tony give you an allowance?'

'No, but he's not mean. He gave me the most beautiful red car for Christmas. He tied it up with yards of white ribbon. He said nobody else in the house could make a nice bow.'

'Hilda can.'

'That's what I thought, but Tony can't abide Hilda.'

'What do you do about buying your frocks and things?'

'Tony's got accounts everywhere that he says he expects me to use. Even at the chemist's.'

'You always smell nice.'

He put his hand on her knee. Blades came in with the post on a silver salver and left it on the telephone table. Edward craned to have a look.

'I wonder who that interesting envelope's for? How splendid that I won't have to answer it,' said Edward.

'How can you tell you won't?'

'Because nobody knows where I'm staying. That's the fun of it. I can come here unbeknownst.'

Angie looked at this ally. Then she got up and inspected the big envelope. 'It's something that might be urgent for Farnley,' she said, and ran out with it.

Blades stayed, winding clocks. Edward still sat on the sofa, trying to read.

'He gets a lot of post for a little boy,' said Blades. 'I daresay he's taking a course in becoming Mr Atlas, like I did. It costs a lot of money. Her ladyship would know the answer.'

Angie came in again and said to Blades, uncertain about giving an order, 'Do you think we could have a hundred-watt bulb for in here the next time you go to the village?'

'That'll be for Mr Edward, my lady?' Blades said. 'He always had a hundred-watt bulb in his pocket for in here, even when he was a lad.'

Edward said in a low voice to Angie, out of Blades' earshot, 'You've a perfect right to *tell* someone to do something. You don't have to *ask*. Though it's like you to. Perhaps I'd need a hundred-and-fifty-watt bulb now, would I? Time tells.'

Blades said sympathetically, 'Better eyes than yours would be worn out with all the book work you've done.'

Angie lay on her stomach to read Volume One of Gibbon's *The Decline and Fall* as near as possible to the dim light over the sofa.

'I've got a torch here you could be going on with, Master Edward,' said Blades, producing one out of his green baize apron. Neither he nor Edward noticed the second slip into childhood talk. It was native to them.

Edward switched the torch on. 'Just the thing. Thanks.' Then he went towards the window where he had been standing, and picked up his books to bring them back to the sofa. He put a book mark in the fine print volume he had been reading and began the last eighth of an Agatha Christie. Angie looked up from the floor and saw his intentness. She held his right ankle, which was in a tartan hand-knitted sock. Blades stepped over her to wind a clock.

'That's the family tartan you're holding, my lady,' Blades said. 'The housekeeper has the pattern. We could ask her to make you a jumper in it.' The reading went on. A clock with a *coloratura* chime struck 1 2 3 4 5 6 7 8 9 10 11 as he wound it. Blades continued the chimes on his fingers. 'New Year's Eve. Well, and there's a bit of ill-luck for you. Thirteen hours exactly till the New Year comes in.'

Clocks started chiming all over the library. Blades collected the keys and put them on his chain. 'Happy New Year, all,' he said. 'As and when it comes.'

Farnley came running into the room and whispered something to Angie.

'This deserves a bottle of champagne,' said Angie, looking excited. 'Blades, could we have some champagne, please? For five. You'll have some? I must leave for a minute. There's something I want to tell Farnley's father.' She went out, but poked her head back around the door. 'And perhaps some ginger beer,' she said to Blades.

Blades said, knowing what was right, 'Could I suggest some Guinness for all instead? Guinness to mix with the champagne. A Black Velvet on New Year's Eve.'

Angie went out again. Blades leaned out of the door after her. 'His lordship was bothering the cook for a lick of the basin and now he's having a lie down,' he said, his head invisible from the room.

'Good news?' said Edward to Farnley, patting the sofa beside him because Farnley had been left standing.

'I won a competition,' said Farnley.

'Congratulations, sir,' said Blades. 'Mind you don't step on her ladyship's book.'

Tony and Angie came in: Tony first, ahead of Angie, kicking the door shut in her face with his heel. 'Sorry, old girl,' he said casually, opening the door behind him to let her in, though without looking back. Edward absorbed all this. So did Farnley, who had a big brown envelope sticking out of his pocket. Angie covered her face with her hands for a moment. Edward watched her. She didn't see. She revived and said, 'Blades, let's get Hilda. And another glass for her, when you bring the tray.'

'I think she's busy with her pigeons, my lady,' said Blades. 'But thank you.'

Blades left. Tony made a sudden vicious dive at Farnley's pocket. The boy was as strong as he was and hung onto the envelope. Blades came back into the room during the struggle, carrying a tray of glasses and a champagne bottle. Tony was shouting at Farnley: 'Give that to me, sir!' he yelled three or four times, in a voice as dry as a water biscuit, the veins on his forehead standing out. Farnley stared at him as they fought. Blades stood immobilized by the door. His hands were shaking so that the glasses rattled on the tray. Tony had his son in a half-nelson and the boy was sinking at the knees. 'It's a *school essay*, Tony,' shouted Angie, running to them. 'He's won a *prize*.' She tried to calm Tony by calming her own voice. She put a hand on his arm and said, 'We should all be celebrating it. We should all be having champagne.'

Tony released Farnley as if he couldn't be bothered with fighting a child, and turned instead on Angie. 'You're lying,' he said. 'Uncle Edward, Angie's lying. Where's the letter to me from the headmaster? I'm going riding.' He went out, slamming the door behind him.

'I can't manage champagne bottles,' said Angie. 'Edward, are you used to them?' She shook Farnley's hand gravely. 'Well done. You will have some?'

'Not when Papa's like this,' said Farnley. He went out, followed by Blades. Angie made a move to follow him but Edward stopped her. 'You were lying to Tony about the essay, weren't you?' he said.

'Farnley's unhappy.'

'Darling girl, but you were lying.'

'Not actually. It was a *sort* of a school prize. A writing school prize. He won twenty-five pounds for a story.'

'Why didn't you tell his father?' Pause. 'No, I do see why you didn't, given Tony.'

'The twenty-five pounds has to be Farnley's pocket money,' she said. 'Tony says he doesn't need pocket money, and I've nothing to give him regularly. It's the regularity one's grateful for. I sold an old fur stole to raise something but second-hand things never bring much, do they? I got five pounds.' She went over to the window. 'He's sold his *Doctor Dolittle* books and his *Children's Encylopedia*. We advertised for a buyer. We had to be very careful not to be traceable.'

'What does he need the money for, though?'

'He told me it was for a flight fund. He said everyone needs a flight fund. He's got everything packed away.' She saw Farnley out of the window. 'He's going somewhere on his bicycle with a knapsack! Edward, where's he going?' She ran out of the room and down stairs, calling, 'Farnley! Farnley!' but the boy was bicycling hard, not wanting to hear her, and she respected his wish.

Twelve midnight. Clocks were chiming all over the house. Angie, Tony and Blades hung over the banisters. The front door banged, and there was the sound of feet on the marble stairs. Edward came up carrying a lump of coal, a penny, and a piece of bread. He gave them to Angie, who kissed him.

'Happy New Year, sir,' said Blades to Edward. 'Happy New Year, my lord,' he said to Tony with a bite in his voice. 'That's wealth, food and warmth for the new year.' He turned to Angie, looking at the coal in her hand, and then at her face. 'Happy New Year, my lady. I'm a bit on the chilly side. It's not the coal we want, of course, it's oil. That Middle East. It's worse than the Balkans when I was a boy. I hardly like to go to bed these days.'

Tony kissed Angie. 'I'm turning in. Let me know about Farnley.'

'Do you want me to come?' said Angie. 'I hung the Gainsborough. As a surprise.'

'Oh?' said Tony distantly. 'I told the estate carpenter to do it.' He disappeared into their bedroom, leaving Edward and Angie together with Blades, who shook both by the hand and went to bed. Edward and Angie arrived in the library, according to their natures.

'Shall we read while you're waiting to hear about Farnley?' said Edward. 'Someone will ring. I used to do this sort of escaping. Most do.'

'I don't understand Tony. We could have taken any calls *together*.'

'Farnley's much more like you than he's like Tony. Isn't that strange. Don't fret.'

After a long while, the phone rang.

'Yes?' said Angie. 'Yes, that's what we guessed. It was the drivers on New Year's Eve I was worried about. 57030, yes, I'm writing it down . . . Do you really think so? He showed me some, but I'm not a writer so I'm no judge. Wish him luck with the play, and ask him if he wants me to drive over with his typewriter . . . Yes, it was a present. The one he had before was like a treadle sewing-machine . . . I must go and tell his father.' She put down the telephone. 'That was his writing school,' she said to Edward. 'His tutor. He had her private address. He'd written to her for it in case of emergency, she said. He's going to stay with her until the term starts. He wants to write a play while he's there.' She went out, but was back in a moment or two. 'Tony's asleep.'

'I thought he would be. Come and sit beside me. Was he snoring?'

'A bit.' Pause. 'How could he go off to sleep? Edward, how could he?'

Edward peered at her and started to use his pocket handkerchief on her face.

'It's all right,' said Angie, grinning. 'I'm not crying this time. I don't like women crying. I'm sorry I did today.'

Edward pushed back her hair from her face and kissed her forehead.

'What a happy New Year, all told,' said Angie. 'What a lucky thing we had you in the house.'

'Why?'

'You being tall and dark, and staying here to be the first to cross the threshold.'

'That's a local custom for us all, isn't it? First-footing on New Year's Eve.'

'You know my family had to leave Newcastle? We don't like the South much but Dad had to find work, and I did fashion modelling. My nose was never right, though.'

'What do you mean, your nose isn't right? You don't really think that? One always finds things out late about people one knows best. Not *too* late for me to learn them is it? Do you want to read?'

Angie had got up, though not to get a book but to put on a record of the Charleston. She was wearing a white fringe dress that swung as she danced. He watched.

'I could teach you the Turkey Trot,' he said.

'Or we could go for a drive in my car?'

'We could do anything. I suppose it isn't possible that you might marry me?'

'Yes.' Pause. 'That's what I was thinking.' She moved to him and held out her hands to him. 'Why not?'

'You're the best thing that's ever happened to me in my life,' said Edward. 'You don't hedge, do you? That's one of the facts about you.' Pause. 'There's Tony.'

Angie had a shot of regret, and then of anger. 'No, there isn't Tony,' she said. 'Not in any way.'

'I'm getting on, of course,' said Edward.

Angie made a move towards him, stirred, holding out her hands. He said cheerfully, 'But you'd make a most beautiful widow. Yves St Laurent would see us both out, wouldn't he? Though some of the best are already gone. Balenciaga.'

'Come for a drive.'

She had moved closer. He took her by one hand and went to the door. She turned off the hundred-watt bulb but he turned it on again. He let her go out first, and then they both sped down the corridor, switching on lights as they went.

Angie drew away beside her bedroom door and looked at Tony's muddy riding boots, left out carelessly for someone to clean.

Edward gripped her hand again, tucking it under his arm like a book. 'Think of the fun we'll have before I kick the bucket,' he said.

A Lovely Bit of Wood

'I feel like doing a spot of work,' said Willy, a retired sergeant who is a carpenter by hobby in his spare time from watching television. When TV closes down, inspiration to work often strikes him. His wife, Doris, stands by at the work-bench in the garden with a torch. He can't carpenter without a mate whatever the day or hour, though she has to get up at six to go to her cleaning jobs on weekdays.

'It's dead of night by now,' said Doris this Saturday. 'You'll wake the neighbours with the hammering when they're wanting a long lie-in. If you start now, you'll go on till dawn.'

'Nothing to all that rock-and-roll next door, and the choir-practice across the road.'

Doris and Willy live in a small London house near the Elephant and Castle. The front room is covered with wallpaper that Willy put up himself in his more robust days. The paper is speckled dark cream, with a deep flowered border at the top and bottom to cover up mistakes in cutting the panels to equal size. Furniture is placed to hide the bubbles in the wallpapering. The carpet is patterned. There is a cocktail cabinet full of cut-glass but without bottles to drink, apart from sweet sherry, and brandy for medicinal purposes. Willy sits mostly in his television armchair with a beer. Doris likes ruby port but she has begun to take out her two false teeth before having it because Willy has said, hoping to make a joke of it, that he can't bring himself to fancy a woman with pink teeth. The room is full of odd pieces of wood and lengths of moulding. Willy has just finished a corner cupboard for shells and mementoes as a birthday present for his son, who has risen in the world and is married to a librarian. The librarian is gently bored by the monthly Sunday visits to her in-laws.

The most beautiful thing in the front room is a marble clock over the fireplace. The fireplace is empty, this part of London now being a smokeless zone and the electricity fire being too big to go into the recess. Willy once measured the cutting that would be needed to accommodate the electric fire and went into the walls with a drill to find out if they were weight-bearing. One of them is. It would be possible to build a pier to carry the weight instead, Willy says: but this one is one of the many problems he has shelved for a moment. Willy bought the marble clock for a shilling at a jumble sale. The inside, visible through the glass sides, is a handsome collaboration of brass cogs and screws and wheels, like an early steam engine. When Willy bought the clock it wouldn't go. He planned to give the job to a jeweller if he couldn't manage it himself. He took the complicated works apart and laid the pieces on a copy of the *Daily Mirror* on the kitchen table, labelled 'Leave these alone.'

'I can't roll out my pastry,' Doris had said, many times.

'You have to think about these things,' Willy had said, many times. 'You don't go rushing into putting a lovely marble clock together as if it was a toaster.'

There is actually also a dismantled toaster, waiting for the right time to be repaired, in the garden shed outside. One Christmas Eve he sat down in front of the pieces on the *Daily Mirror* and patiently put the clock together again. It keeps perfect time. Two pieces of the machinery remain a mystery. There is nowhere for them to fit. They are wrapped in newspaper in a honey jar, labelled, 'Pieces of marble clock, unused', in the garden shed.

Willy's and Doris' back garden is a show of roses for the first six feet, hampered by a coal bunker that was provided by the authorities in the Second World War and that was always too small. Willy built another one, wonderfully bigger, with the correct sloping roof, and a hinged loading hole of his own invention that made rain water drain through the joins in the hinges onto the coal that was then, before the area became a smokeless zone, supposed to be kept dry inside it. The openings of both of the now fuel-free bunkers are just big enough to take the pieces of wood that Willy never throws away, tea trays that need varnishing, the old handlebars of their son's tricycle that might, Willy says, come in useful, three pram wheels (the fourth mysteriously not findable) stolen by Willy from a disused Go-Kart contraption made of an orange crate and wheels that he found abandoned on a dust-heap, and a rusty bird cage of which only the plastic bottom frill to keep the seed from falling out is still intact.

The workshop, at the back of a small concrete area, is the garden shed. On the back wall there are shelves of jam jars, pickle jars, and bouillon cube jars that are used for storing nails and screws, labelled 'inch-tens', 'flathead nails', 'panel pins', 'two-inch nails', and 'countersunk screws'. They are sealed with tape, which Willy feels prevents the nails growing rusty. He doesn't like the damp in the garden, though it is good for his roses. He has fixed a tarpaulin over the entrance to the shed. That took him six months' of thought: how to attach the tarpaulin so that it would neither tear in the wind nor detract from the look of the roses. Inside the shed, again on the back wall, there is also a pegboard with saws arranged in order of size, chisels in oiled rags, pinchers, pliers, screwdrivers (plain and Phillips), and hammers hanging in a scaled row like a xylophone. In smaller jars there are washers and leatherwork nails for cobbling shoes. His work-bench, to speak formally, is beneath these useful things, but it can't actually be worked at, although it is hypothetically ideal, because of the clutter around it and the permanence of its attachment. It is made of a heavy old door, immovable on account of the workmanship that went into fixing it to the back wall. The front legs are made of lengths of wood two inches by four inches (two b'fours). There is no room to work at it owing to the rotting deckchairs in front of it, which are considered by Willy still to have some life left in them, and the two bikes that his son had as a boy. The parents are too fond of the bikes to junk them. There is also an old chest of drawers that Willy insists on hanging on to – 'In case of crisis, with the whole shooting-match here,' he says, darkly implying that his daughter-in-law might move in any day, and the grandchildren too. The now grown-up son's discarded first moped is kept out in the rain under a plastic sheet.

So the top of the smaller bunker is Willy's work-bench. He inverts the lid of the bunker so that the handle goes downwards to give himself an even surface. Even so, it has to be said that the lid as a whole goes at an awkward slope. He uses the smaller bunker instead of the larger surface of his own bunker because the concrete of the one originally supplied is actually better to hammer on, and also because his special hinged lid can't be turned upside down to get rid of the handle. The work-bunker is in front of a dovecote that he built his wife as a tenth wedding anniversary present, pinning up an old blackout curtain at the kitchen window so that Doris wouldn't see what he was doing, and also managing without her as his mate so as to be able to surprise her. He stands on a piece of hall carpet that Doris found to keep his feet warm. He wears a long brown coat with pockets for cigarettes and nails and rulers, partly because things are apt to slide off the bunker. There is a saw-horse beside him, but everything except sawing has to be done on top of the bunker. Things are checked with a spirit level on the floor on the concrete area. He once made a beautiful sideboard that he swears is dead true. But it wobbled indoors when he first carved the Sunday joint, throwing grease onto the wallpaper where the fat spreads as if on blotting paper.

'The floors of this house aren't level,' Willy complained

bitterly. So Doris cut down two vinegar bottle corks to prop up two of the legs.

'Those bits of cork are an insult,' Willy said to her this weekend. 'I'd got it right on the concrete down to the last T. You saw me slaving away. I made sure the concrete itself was level before I began, with bits of wood under newspapers.' He held the back of his waist.

'There's something wrong with you,' said Doris, using wariness because Willy was panicked by doctors.

'I've got my eye on your spice jars,' said Willy. 'It's not the sort of thing you'd thing of, but they'll do beautifully for some little upholstery pins I have in mind.'

'The grandchildren are coming to tea. I need the caraway seed that's in the thyme jar for the cake.'

'To hell with the cake.'

'You'd say that about your own grandchildren? Besides, your daughter-in-law has a liking for caraway seed.'

'Stuck-up bitch.'

'She's not stuck-up, she's well read.' Doris looked at the wall-to-wall carpeting in the front room, which was protected by rugs that spoiled the look but saved the footmarks, and wished she were more of a reader. 'I could be more of a reader, if I had the time,' she said under her breath.

'You can't be, with your cooking and your herb-growing and me. I hope it isn't me.'

'Of course it isn't, dear.'

'I expect it's the herbs that take it out of you. You're always giving away cuttings.'

'Is Billy staying the night tomorrow?'

'Marion's got to go back,' said Doris. 'Billy starts work late on a Monday but she's got to be at work by nine.'

Willy snorted. 'Librarian!'

'It's because of the children, not only because of her work. It's important, of course. Her work.'

'Billy might stay, though, if we asked him, mightn't he? Like the old days.'

'Time's got to move on, Willy,' said Doris.

'You could make him one of your fish pies.'

'You like it when Billy stays the night, don't you?'

'Of course I do. He's my son.'

'We had him *together*, the *two* of us, so it stands to reason I'd like him to stay too, doesn't it?'

'A man's his father's son.'

'You like it because you've got an excuse to give up your half

94

of the bed to the kids and sleep down here where it's warmer.'

'It's warmer here because of the kitchen. The bedrooms are like ice. I expect that's what's brought on my problem. If I have one, which I doubt. Doctors are all right but I don't trust hospital staff. I think I'll go and do a bit of work, as I said.'

'Sit down and watch the posh channel on the BBC for a while. They've got a special late programme.'

'I can't seem to cultivate an interest in the BBC tonight,' said Willy loftily. 'Where's my clothes prop?'

'Propping up the washing line, for once. Doing what it should be doing.'

'You know I need it for my work.'

'Couldn't you get another clothes prop?'

'Clothes props don't grow on trees,' said Willy with a sage look.

Doris thought of saying they were made out of them, but decided the remark might make him think of Marion, and instead went and made a caraway seed cake to make use of staying up, fitting it in with long bouts of standing near Willy in the dark while he worked on his new project. It was a bookcase to be given as a golden anniversary present to their best friends. Willy always had to have a mate when he was working: someone who wouldn't advise, someone to encourage him.

When his grandchildren, whom he adored, came the next day, he measured their hair with one of his folding rulers. They giggled with their hands up to their mouths, being of an age to be absorbed by teeth. One of them looked at a flight of china ducks on the wall.

'Do ducks have teeth?' the child said, lisping through the front gap in his mouth.

'No,' said Willy.

'Maybe,' said Doris. 'Maybe long ago, when we were all brontosauruses and amoebas.'

'No,' said Marion, 'amoebae never had teeth.'

'The wife might be right. How can you be sure about bygones?' said Willy. 'Stay the night, Billy?'

'It's so cold in my old room always.'

'Mother's put in a new oil heater in the hall to take the chill off the upstairs,' said Willy.

'Otherwise Mother hasn't done very well,' said Doris about herself, to cheer up Marion over the duck question. Marion was eating cake with her little finger crooked.

'In what haven't you done well?' said Marion.

'Because I did the washing yesterday and it means opening the manhole because otherwise the drain doesn't flow away properly, and it stopped Willy getting on with his work today.'

'The place was sopping,' said Willy. 'Mother always wants to do her washing just when I have to do my work. Wet towels flapping round my tools and no clothes pole. Children, look what I made for you, in spite of your grandmother.' He gave them some rather ugly, beautifully made jewellery boxes with the initials of the children carved on them.

'They're lovely handles,' said Marion. There was a pause. Willy got up and said, picking up one of his wife's china Bambis from the corner cupboard, 'Mother found them on her way to work.'

'One of them doesn't match,' said an observant four-year-old.

'We'll see to that,' said Willy.

'It doesn't matter. I quite like it,' said the child.

'It's just *temporary*,' said Willy.

'What are you making now?' said Marion, pretending interest.

'He's making a bookcase for our friends' golden wedding anniversary,' said Doris.

'The jewellery boxes need staining,' said Willy. 'I'll get around to it when I can get the right stain. You can't rush these things. And then the polishing. I thought the box would do for the boy's future collar studs.'

'You never quite finish anything, Dad,' said Billy.

'Yes, he does,' said Doris.

'What about the strip in the kitchen that he never finished painting for you?' Billy said.

'He got interested in something else,' said Doris.

'Television,' said Marion.

'This golden wedding present,' said Willy, ignoring her. 'The warped wood you get now's disgusting.'

'What about the two-foot-six piece you had in the hall? That's been in lovely condition for years,' said Billy.

'I wanted two-foot-eight,' said Willy.

'So?' said Marion.

There was a pause. 'So?' said Marion.

'Your mother-in-law went off on her bicycle to get it cut. She had it tied to the bicycle. Nothing difficult about it. The shelves we had in the bunker. Just as well I'd kept them. They hadn't warped after all those years. We bring them indoors in the damp weather,' said Willy.

Doris went out to make some more tea. 'Don't tell her,' said Willy, 'but I've got another lovely bit of wood for a surprise to hold china in that alcove. Not a flaw in it.'

'What size?' said Billy. 'Home carpenters never believe their own wood warps. Is it warped?'

'Oh, it's a big alcove if you move the cocktail cabinet and the three-piece a bit.'

'I expect that's why she's moved them,' said Billy.

'She keeps rearranging things. Women do,' said Willy. 'I found her using the clothes prop and it was holding something I'd just glued.'

'What does she use as an ironing board when you've got your carpentry on it?' said Marion.

'She likes the dining-room table. She uses eight blankets and an old sheet so as not to spoil the varnish. You couldn't call her a careless woman. She gives a lot of thought to things.'

Doris came in with the tea. Willy said, 'We were talking about ironing, dear. She often uses a flat-iron for my sake because she doesn't want it to get rusty and you never know when you might be without electricity. Look at the blackout they had in New York. Look at the mischief that did.'

'You shouldn't let your wife cook and work and get your timber for you,' said Marion.

Billy said, 'Obsolete things exist strangely in women, side by side with anarchy and innovation.' Willy gave him a hard glance and said, 'Don't you go speaking to your mother like that.'

'Your father misses his work-shed,' said Doris.

'Garden shed.'

'If it's a garden shed, that's my fault. I let the vines grow up it,' said Doris.

'She's proud of them,' said Billy to Willy. 'And rightly.'

'They block the light,' said Willy.

'The windows are only sixteen inches square and they're frosted,' said Billy. 'No wonder you can't see.'

'Eighteen by eighteen,' said Willy. 'You helped me put them in when you were a boy. About ten, you were. I wonder you don't remember the measurements.'

'That was a long time ago, dear,' said Doris. 'He hasn't got your memory.'

'He always remembered to water your cactuses,' said Willy.

'Cacti,' said Marion. The telephone went. Marion answered.

'She's used to the telephone, of course, being a librarian,' said Willy.

'I can't get accustomed to it,' said Doris.

'One of her gentlemen had it put in,' said Willy. 'I always said it was an unnecessary expense but her gentleman said he needed to be able to get hold of her.'

'It's the hospital,' said Marion to Willy. 'It's for you.'

'Put it down, girl.' There was a pause, and he stamped his foot and had a swig of beer in the kitchen. 'No call to answer if you don't want to.'

'What does your husband *do* all day?' asked one of Doris's employers the next Thursday, worried that a woman of sixty-eight was working to support a tired husband of sixty-four. The employer (Doris' longest-lived, and her favourite) was a tall, stooping man called Roger Borthwick who worked at the Stock Exchange.

'He's a carpenter by hobby,' said Doris proudly, covering her teeth. She giggled and said, 'Excuse my teeth.'

'You should get them seen to,' said Mr Borthwick.

'I'm all right,' said Doris. When she came in to look after his flat every week, she left him notes written on his old laundry lists saying she was in the pink and hoped that this found him as it left her at present.

'We're going back to the dentist next week, and he's going to see us right about nice new sets. You won't recognize me then,' said Doris. She went on polishing the silver. 'My grandfather had a lovely silver tray given to him when he retired. Willy didn't get anything from his job because he left on sick leave.'

'I didn't know he'd been ill? I thought it was just his teeth that bothered him.'

'There's something wrong with him, Mr Borthwick, but he won't talk about it. I tell you, it's like getting a cat into a bath, dragging him near a doctor. I'd need an anaesthetic for him to get him to hospital, that's what. Just as well all his teeth came out at once. The dentist sized him up. He said to me quietly on Monday, "Give you any trouble, getting him here?" Clever men, dentists. He was someone you could trust. I took him on one side and said, "If I was you, I'd take them all out at one go while you're about it because I'll never get him here again." Then I had a think to myself and said, "You could take the rest of mine out at the same time, to encourage him." He gave me a bit of a look and then he looked at Willy, sitting in the dentist's chair and hanging onto the arms for dear life as if it was tipping backwards, and he had a see into my mouth, and said he thought it wasn't a bad idea. Willy wanted me to stay in the room with him, so the dentist had me there to calm him down.'

'Then you had yours out. Alone, I suppose.'

'Well, it's easier for a woman. Willy was recovering.'

'*And* you take him out for a walk to get him away from television even when you must be flat out from work.'

'He couldn't go by himself. He won't even go to the post box by himself, though he'll nip out for a beer or some smokes if I've forgotten to get them. He's only really happy with his carpentry.'

'That was a lovely pin-case he made for me.'

'I told him you didn't have pins, being a bachelor, but he said it would be just as useful for collar studs. He was dead set on doing something dainty for once, but his real talent is for the big jobs.' She made a large gesture in the air with her silver-polishing duster. 'Bed-heads, cocktail cabinets; things on that scale.' She put down the duster, dipped a toothbrush into a saucer of silver polish and started cleaning a Georgian flower-vase. 'I'm looking forward to the day when I can use one of these again, I have to admit. A toothbrush.' Doris laughed once more with her hand over her mouth. 'The dentist said I mustn't laugh because it would make the lines heavier. Do the lines show?'

'I wish you wouldn't work so hard,' said Mr Borthwick. 'The place is like a new pin every Thursday.'

'You're the cleanest man I ever knew. There's nothing to do here but polish the brass and the silver and re-make the bed. I can tell when your girlfriend's been here, if you'll excuse my saying so. She doesn't know the fringe on the bedspread belongs at the bottom.'

'You still work too hard, considering all you do with Willy to look after.'

'It's true he hasn't been himself since his teeth started playing him up, but he's no trouble usually.'

'But you both had them out at the same time, and you're making no fuss.'

'I give him nice mashed potatoes and cream of wheat. Nothing to chew.' Doris put one hand up to her face and the other up to her new permanent wave and giggled shyly.

'Talk of lines on someone's face. His mouth has quite fallen in.'

'I don't notice yours has. Especially with your new hat.'

'You know, Mr Borthwick, Willy said, "For the Lord's sake, go and get yourself a hat with a veil, and a new permanent, until the National Health Service decides to get off its you-know-what." In the meantime I can see his mouth collapsing and I worry it'll never come out again, but he's not one for looking in the mirror so he don't trouble.'

'You wouldn't let me send you to my dentist?'

'What, the both of us?' Doris looked frightened. 'There's only one thing as grand as a doctor you pay and that's a dentist you pay. I wouldn't like any dentist of yours to see me in this condition. Besides, guineas don't grow on trees.'

'It would be on my bill, if you wouldn't mind.'

'That wouldn't be right.'

'Willy should be earning like you Doris. He should be going out to work.'

'He enjoys his television. I get him up in the morning and give him a nice cup of tea and he generally sits there in the front room till I'm back from work. Then we go out for a walk. And he's got his carpentry.'

'But you're older than he is.'

'Yes, but he carries more weight here,' Doris patted her stomach. 'He envies me my stomach muscles. He says his are in a bad way because of the cups of tea he has all day. The doctor told him a cup every two hours to wash out his kidneys.' Her hands unconsciously moved round to her back and she stretched, imagining what it was to be Willy.

'His trouble isn't kidneys, it's sitting in front of the television set all the time. It's not right, your doing three jobs a day and then even taking him out for a walk when you get back,' said Mr Borthwick.

'The doctor said it was bad for his constitution, having to sit so much.'

'He doesn't have to sit. It's bad for you, *walking* so much.'

'His face is falling in.' Doris put a tea cloth up to her mouth and laughed again. 'Excuse me, but people look comical after anaesthetics for teeth. Like bicycle tubes that have had the air let out. Luckily I couldn't see myself. The dentist said it was better not to look.'

'Shouldn't you have new sets put in? Won't your jaws shrink without false teeth?'

Next Thursday she telephoned Mr Borthwick at seven o'clock in the morning. 'I'm ever so sorry, but there's something wrong. No, it's not me, it's Willy. But we've got our new teeth. You've got to look on the bright side. I'll be in later if I can.'

When Borthwick came back from the Stock Exchange that evening he found Doris crying and polishing the silver.

'Hoping you're not surprised to see me, Mr Borthwick,' she said.

'What's happened?'

'Wouldn't you know. It was no sooner we got our teeth than Willy had to go to the emergency department at hospital. A man on a bicycle came as early as the milk. It had crossed my mind that Willy carrying on about not being able to move might be all psychological, what's the word? I mean, all in his mind, because he doesn't think his teeth are up to mine. But an emergency's an emergency, and there was a man on a bicycle with a letter in black and white. Danger of internal bleeding, it said. "Well, I'm not going," he said. You know what he is about hospitals. "And haven't you got an empty jar, mother?" he said. "A nice big one, because I've got a pound and a half of lovely new panel pins and they're spilling out of the brown paper all over the garden shed." So I got him his jam jar. It was a pickle jar, as a matter of fact. And he pottered out to the garden, and by the time he came back I'd got his suitcase packed and I said, "It's all done." "I'm not going," he said, sitting down in front of the telly and doing a bit of his tongue-and-grooving work with his hammer and chisel. It was a lovely bit of wood even if there were shavings all over the nice clean carpet. "Your packing's all done," I said, "and we're going." "I've got my work to do," he said. "Besides, you haven't cleaned my teeth." '

'You clean his *teeth* for him, on top of everything else?'

'He says cleaning's my forte. I do the two sets at once. I'd soaked them overnight and given them back to him in the early morning but they wouldn't do for him. He said he wasn't going to hospital with breakfast on his teeth. I'd only just scrubbed them but he's a stickler for etiquette. Anyway, I said he wasn't going to *have* any breakfast if he was going to hospital. They don't like patients who are outside of their breakfasts.'

'You're cleaning all day, and then you clean two sets of teeth?'

'The trouble was getting him to budge. Anyway, I cleaned his teeth again for peace and did my own for luck and we arrived at the hospital, me carrying his suitcase because of the danger of the bleeding, and I said, "He's here for his emergency." They looked him up and down at reception, and I got him a cup of water, and the lady said, "Didn't you get our telegram saying there's been a mistake about the tests? We thought you mightn't have," she said, "so we sent a letter of confirmation." Willy was as white as a sheet and said, very quick and decided, like as if he was back in the army, "We haven't had no telegrams and no letter." Then he said to me in a hurry, "Best we be going." The lady said, not knowing all the trouble of getting him there, that it was just as well because there was a ward strike and all the male orderlies was off. Willy doubled up. "Is he in pain?" asked the lady. "We'll get one of the registrars." We waited and waited and Willy wouldn't be examined without me. He said I was his wife, after all. So this nice young man, very spruce but worn out, I should say, did a lot of knocking on Willy's waist and Willy did a lot of howling and said he'd had trouble enough with his teeth without his kidneys coming into it, and the doctor said he thought it was probably tension, and Willy hit him. So then the nice young man saw us out, and Willy said he was sorry, and as we was going home on the bus Willy and I talked about what to do about his jam jars for nails. He said he was short of jars and it was all very well but you couldn't be a professional without the right number and size of jam jars.'

When Doris got home from work there was still no telegram and no letter. But a policeman did arrive on a bicycle. He took off his driving gloves and stood there in the front room, sounding perturbed in his rubbery mackintosh.

'Aren't you hot in that? What about a glass of beer?' said Doris.

'Your husband is wanted in hospital,' said the policeman.

'We've just been,' said Willy firmly.

'They tried to telephone after you left,' said the policeman, 'allowing enough time for you to get back on the bus, but they say the phone can't be in working order. They're going to report it.'

'How did they get the number?' said Willy. 'I'm not going.'

'The hospital says it's an emergency, and would you sign this?'

'It can't be an emergency,' said Doris, crying, and pouring a bottle of beer for the policeman. 'The form says five days' time.'

'Emergencies work slowly. Thank you, but I don't drink on the job,' said the policeman.

'This isn't a job,' said Willy. 'It's a jaunt, so long as it isn't *your* emergency. My wife would understand me. Emergency, they say! Five days!'

'Not a jaunt. Not in this rain,' said the policeman.

'No, I see that,' said Willy.

'You're soaked through your mac. You'll catch your death if you don't have something to line your stomach,' Doris said to the policeman, who had a piece of caraway seed cake. Then he left, getting a signature by proxy from Doris. Willy tried to escape from trouble by going out to the pub, and told Doris triumphantly when he came back that it was no wonder they hadn't had the telegram because he'd seen a telegraph delivery boy burning piles of yellow telegraph-office envelopes in a back yard. 'To keep himself warm, he said it was,' said Willy.

'I just had a *ring* from hospital to confirm you,' said Doris.

'What did you want to go and answer for?'

'It might have been urgent. It was.'

'*Emergency* again, I suppose,' said Willy fiercely, scared.

'They'd found out we had a working telephone after all. They were a bit cross about the policeman coming round unnecessary. I told them it couldn't be that urgent if they only wanted you in five days' time, and the doctor laughed, and said you was to try heat. You sleep down here in the warm tonight.'

'It's my kidneys. There's nothing they can tell me about my kidneys. I had them go wrong in the War and it was just the same.'

'I daresay it's working in the cold by the bunker,' said Doris.

'Casting aspersions on my bunker.'

'I don't mean *your* bunker. I mean the small one they sent us in the War. You go to bed on the couch with a nice hot-water bottle.'

'Where'll you be?'

'I'll sleep in your television chair. I might not hear you from upstairs if I go deep out.'

'A chair's no place to sleep.'

'It'll be cosy enough with the ironing blankets. I can bring them in from the airing cupboard.'

Hours later, only two before she had to go work, he woke up sighing. She was over to him in a moment with a glass of warm water and an aspirin. Then she telephoned the hospital, fingering a carved pill box Willy had made her, though she wasn't one for pills. 'It'll do for your hat pins,' he said. It was funny that all these years of marriage hadn't made him notice that she didn't use hat pins.

'Doctor, he's groaning, and the heat doesn't seem to help him.'

'Has he got a hot-water bottle?' said the medical resident at the hospital, tired as a dog.

'I'll refill it. Lord, the hours you work,' said Doris on the telephone.

'You could give him a cup of tea every two hours.'

'The trouble is that I've got to go out to work soon.'

'Couldn't he make it himself?'

'He doesn't bestir himself much when I'm out.'

'What does he like?'

'Television.'

'What else?'

'I think he quite likes me coming home after work.'

'How many hours a day do you do?'

'Nine or ten, and then there's the buses.'

'He should be out and about more. His kidneys will pack up.'

She started to press the hinge of Willy's box open and then said, 'Oh, pardon me, doctor. I've gone and broken his hinge.'

'What?'

'His hinge. He's a very gifted home carpenter but he likes to take his time. I'd best get this box round the corner to a repair shop before he notices.'

'Tell him to come in and see me.'

'He won't doctor. He took a taxi home from the bus stop after hospital yesterday when they made a mess of his appointment. I've never known him take a taxi.'

'You say heat doesn't help.'

'He's not making a fuss, doctor. I can tell. It's bothering him.'

'If heat doesn't help, try ice.'

A while later a second policeman knocked at the door. Doris went to open it. Willy got up and peeked through the net curtains.

'Don't let him in,' he said, but it was too late.

'Have a cup of tea,' Doris said in the hall. Willy tried to bar the door of the front room. Doris came in from the hall, pushing the door against his weight.

'He's come about my kidneys.'

'No, he hasn't. That was just a nasty cold you had.'

'It's the hospital, I tell you.'

'Let him in.'

The young policeman stood and twisted his helmet in his hands. 'We're carrying out an all-night investigation of two hundred and fifty letters that have gone astray by clandestine means in the neighbourhood,' he said.

'Nothing for here's gone astray,' said Willy.

'There was a letter from the hospital that never arrived,' said Doris. 'Or they said they'd sent it.'

'Aha,' said the policeman.

Willy went into the kitchen. Doris followed and said, 'He's only doing his job.'

'First telegrams and now letters. Suppose I'd had an appendix?'

'I'd never have got you there.'

'Suppose I'd been in screaming agony?'

Doris went into the front room again, and came back to Willy five minutes later when the policeman had gone. She sat down on the kitchen table.

'I'm making an early start,' said Willy, feigning haste. 'Mind youself on the hand drill, sitting there.' He busied himself. 'Do you know, the day after I saw the boy burning the telegrams, I was out for some smokes and I ran into a postman burning a postbag and warming his hands over an incinerator because he said he didn't feel up to the delivery. Lazy, that's what he was. And not a young man either. My age. Doris, you work too hard. I've been thinking. It's not right, you working for all those young men all day while I'm watching television.'

'You've got your carpentry. I wonder what was in the letter. Of course, hospitals are all psychicological now.'

'They need to be, if working men are going to start burning telegrams and letters that might be urgent.'

That night, with Willy sitting in front of the television set and wheezing with pain as his favourite commercial station was going off the air, Doris filled a hot-water bottle with the frost that collected under the top of the refrigerator, which was old, and always seemed to need defrosting.

'What's this?' Willy asked when she gave him the bottle. 'It's all cold.'

'The doctor said if the heat wasn't helping, try ice.'

Willy flung the ice-pack water bottle at the kitchen door and asked her to watch a late-night BBC arts programme with him, thinking to appeal to her taste, which he secretly thought a bit above his own.

'It's about Italian films,' he said. 'You liked *Three Coins in a Fountain*.'

Iron Larks

Professor Philip Scrope and Professor Nora Scrope sat together in their study in front of a photostat of the human brain. In the old days, before Philip and Nora married, a medieval Scots crucifix belonging to Philip's parents had hung there, for the family had been Presbyterian and God still lingered somewhere in the back of the younger Scropes' heads. The deity is not so easily dislodged. The photostat was lit by a surgical arc lamp that a stringent acquaintance had given them as a Christmas present. On the mantlepiece were seashells from their honeymoon in Majorca, a muddle of photographs, a child's Georgian silver rattle, and a half-eaten peach from the warm greenhouse where Philip liked to potter. The mantlepiece contradicted the photostat.

Philip and Nora, encyclopedically informed, devoted to each other, with gaps of abstractedness about what they hadn't yet had time for and wished to know, were eating cress sandwiches with Professor Pemberton Johnson. He was talking about a Greek writer imprisoned in Athens.

'The Amnesty people say he'll die if we don't get him out, because of his liver. We should do something. After all, he is a great poet.'

'Would it make any difference if he were a bad poet?' said Nora. 'Or not a poet at all?'

'Sometimes you speak as if you didn't really care about literature,' Pemberton said, staring at her beadily and disregarding the evidence of the room, which had piles of books everywhere.

'Has anyone seen my socks?' Philip asked. 'And then shall we go into the greenhouse?' He lumbered up and looked for his socks.

Pemberton said rather irritably to Nora, 'Go and get him another pair.'

'No,' said Philip, 'the particular socks I'm looking for have my garters on them. You'd recognize them in a second by the garters if you'd care to give a hand.'

Pemberton stayed in his chair and went on talking about military dictatorships while Nora and Philip combed the desks and the piles of magazines and books. 'We can send another letter to *The Times*. It's all we seem to be able to do,' said Nora.

Philip stood in the middle of the room and thought more generally. He was a big man, with a heavy head that often wavered as if it were hung on gimbals. He looked sorrowful. 'One expected better of Greece,' he said.

'We're all on the wrong track,' he said.

Pemberton said with contempt, 'You're bogged down by domesticity,' because he took her to be talking about the socks, but she went on, 'Even welfare democracies still try to solve the problem of poverty by keeping the poor alive, often until a very advanced and lonely age.'

'You have a curious dislike of the research intellect. For an intellectual,' Pemberton said.

'Oh no,' Nora said. 'Not of the research intellect. Not of the medical.'

'What she means is that we're not going about things in the right way, politically speaking,' said Philip. 'Not by a complicated enough way of thinking. You don't win the game by sweeping the chessmen off the table.'

Nora found his socks.

'So where were they?' Pemberton moved about in his chair.

'Behind the *Economists*. I think he must have taken them off to do some filing.'

'To do some filing?'

'Well, we've got a rug in front of the filing cabinets for warmth, and anyway I expect one feels freer without socks.'

Philip is a man with mild and expressive eyes who long ago, after Oxford, had so disliked competitive academic minds that he had even given up political scholarship. He had become a route planner for the Automobile Association. He got the sack there after planning a scenic route for a woman motorist who wanted to drive from London to Godalming, a matter of thirty-odd miles. Cherishing a minor dislike of the genteel ways of Godalming and a considerable love of the English country, he sent her via Lewes, which lies out of the way, and then via Stonehenge and Dorchester, which are even more out of the way. The journey took her four days because she was a poor driver and, as she said, interested in scenery. Then the planning of the route came to light, and that Friday Philip lost his job. Not greatly pained, because he was about to marry Nora, he got a job washing up at a Lyons Corner House to keep himself, and began to practise political economy and gardening. He also painted: exquisite little watercolours of flowers, done with a magnifying glass and tiny sable brushes. His nature was unwaveringly to the left, like Nora's. He fought in the Spanish Civil War. By 1939, though he had been one of the prophetic campaigners against fascism, he decided not to fight again. He went to prison as a conscientious objector, allowed out finally on condition that he become a farm labourer. This only reversed his interests: it allowed him to be in the country in the day and to read politics in the evening. Nora often had to leave him then because she was in the Wrens. She looked wonderful in her uniform, he thought. The nipped jacket, the peaked hat, the salute.

Their godchild, Johnny, aged five and a half was upstairs now. Pottering about and thinking, much like Philip and Nora.

'What are you doing, Johnny?' Nora shouted to him.

There was a pause, and then the boy shouted back, 'I'm doing something in the corridor, but I don't know what it's called.'

'This is what linguistics are about,' Pemberton muttered, with affection for linguistics. 'What are you doing it with?' he shouted.

'A magnet and iron filings.'

'That's called physics,' shouted Pemberton. 'But it doesn't matter as long as you're doing it. Come down when you've finished.'

Pemberton got on with people like Johnny. It was sophisticates who bothered him. This was one of the several things the Scropes regarded him for. Clever people made him anxious. Confused, he had fled to America at the beginning of the Second World War and stayed on to work secretly for the CIA. There had been some scandal when the CIA connection came to light, because he had always been revered publicly as the staunch and clear-eyed radical that he so appealingly looked to be, having a tall, schoolboyish, stooping frame and sculptor's eyes. The Scropes were two of the few who still accepted him on his visits back to England.

Nora was thinking of Philip's passion for his old car. It had occurred to her that he might want to go for a drive, and she went outside to warm up the engine.

'What did you do in lessons today?' Pemberton said when Johnny came down.

'History and geography and nature.'

'What's history?'

'People fighting.'

'Tell me what geography is.'

'Where all of you have been.'

'What's nature?'

'Fighting.'

'You said history was fighting.'

'History is people fighting. Nature's animals fighting.'

Philip stopped reading *The Economist*. He had one sock on and one off. 'Oh, the futility of human effort,' he said about some leader he had been absorbed by, though using his accustomed robust voice.

'What about a muffin all round?' said Pemberton. 'I'm afraid they've got a bit cold.'

'I like cold muffins,' said Johnny.

'So do I. Though on the other hand, what about my making you some French toast?'

'What's French toast?' said Johnny.

'French toast is American,' said Pemberton.

'Are you in a muddle?'

Pierced, because the exactness of the question was obvious to Pemberton in a large-ranging way he didn't like to contemplate, the man took the child into the kitchen and began to make French toast for the two of them.

Philip followed. 'You like America, don't you?'

'Well, it's very interesting from the radical point of view,' Pemberton said. 'Very important. A lot of good souls going to prison or thinking things out. But I find I can't get on with any hobbies in New York. I keep hoping for an event to happen. One event a day. Two is too much. But no one can be expected to get through the time without one.'

'I found the same,' said Philip. 'In Europe, now, days pass without an occasion. Shall we have the French toast in the greenhouse?'

Happy among the tomatoes, Philip took out his paints.

Pemberton looked at the canvas on the easel. 'It's very big,' he said.

'I still do miniatures, but I got interested by the size of this particular canvas when I saw it in the shop,' Philip said. 'I go at it in the mornings.'

Nora came back from the garage. The car had eventually started. She looked with engrossment at the mess of green and blue on the canvas. 'He's moving into a splashy period,' she said.

Pemberton was their great friend but intimidated by their simplicity. Beside their agreeable intransigence he felt a truckler. His own contorted political history lurked in his memory. He sat there in the greenhouse and found himself resenting Philip with all his heart.

'Where was it we first met?' said Philip, stirring brushes with big movements in a saucepan of turpentine. Nora left the greenhouse to take Johnny out to his parents, whom she could hear at the door coming to pick him up.

'On the liner to America, wasn't it?' said Pemberton, his ducking out of the Second World War uppermost in his mind.

'No, I think it was at Yale.'

'Oh yes, of course. When was it? I remember it.'

'McCarthy reign. I'd come over to lecture.'

'That's right.'

'You dined with us, and everything was splendid except that you got into a tiff with a woman professor about the House Un-American Activities Committee. You said you were against it, and she said you weren't.'

'I remember. It was an interesting evening.'

'I thought it was foul,' Philip said, painting.

'I know what you mean. For me it was actually rather foul, too, but what's the point of making a meal of the past?'

The past happens over and over again if you don't, Philip thought. 'Foul in what way?' he said.

'Why did you think it was foul?' said Pemberton.

Philip came to a decision. 'Two of your students at the table seemed to have been primed I was a Socialist. I was there to be baited. I had an uncomfortable feeling it was *you* who primed them. Did you?'

'Good heavens, no.'

'They showed me letters of yours afterwards that suggested it.'

'I don't believe it.'

'Never mind.'

'What were their names?' asked Pemberton in a fright, thinking to pursue the sort of fact he knew his friend wouldn't remember.

'Look,' Philip said, 'you were on another side then, that's all. You've forgotten what happened. You sometimes blot things out. When you asked me there to lecture, you were in a bad position because you'd changed your nationality and McCarthy was apt to call you a Communist. Wasn't that it? You asked me there because you needed a piece of old fish to throw him, something to fob him off with. Wasn't that it? And I wasn't American, so I didn't suffer. How did you come to do it, though?' There was a pause. 'Were you scared?'

'All I did was ask my students which professor they'd most like to meet,' said Pemberton, stubborn in evasion.

Philip painted large and put aside a bit of French toast.

'Perhaps you're right,' Pemberton said.

'Oh, my dear friend, everyone understands being scared,' Philip said. 'But you can't say perhaps I'm right like that. You could stand up for yourself against me, you know. You do about other things.'

Pemberton stalked about the greenhouse in a rage. 'Your tomatoes are coming along,' he said.

'They're Nora's, really. She takes the trouble over them.'

'I didn't know she liked greenhouses.' Anything to get away from the fifties.

Philip looked at his old friend and said, 'Nora's just come out of a crash course in Russian. I think she's rather whacked.'

'I thought her subjects were Middle English and the sixteenth century.'

'Well, she suddenly got interested in a late-nineteenth-century Russian playwright where there was some miscarriage of justice. She'd been offered the English sixteenth century and she could have made a packet, I suppose, but she decided she wanted to learn something new and stuck out for her nineteenth-century idea. She lost with the board this year, that was the trouble. Her way of doing things doesn't always come out right. But it does often enough. And quantitative judgments aren't the nub of it, of course. If you look at things from that point of view, one thing done right is quite enough for a lifetime, and she's done a great many more than one. Then she seemed tired and I took her to Trinidad because we decided to blow some loot, and she grew interested in ant-eaters. There's a botanical garden there that has a most beautiful pair of ant-eaters. She has an unusual capacity to get interested.'

Nora came out into the greenhouse again and stood against a rare but hardy peach tree, reading.

'What's the book?' said Pemberton.

She didn't hear and went on reading.

Pemberton had an unsteadying flash of insight that everything about himself was gimcrack today. It was a familiar feeling, tacitly known by the Scropes, that he tried not to harbour for long. He began to make a plan.

'She doesn't hear when she's concentrating,' said Philip. 'Nor do you, sometimes.'

Pemberton resented the last word. 'I have to keep alert,' he said.

'Ear to the ground,' said Philip agreeably. 'You've always been good at that. You don't mind my messing about like this while we're talking?'

'I wouldn't call it messing about. I'd call it painting,' said Pemberton with too much effusion. He hated himself when he overdid things.

Philip felt shy for his friend, who then said importantly, 'We were talking about Greece, but what about England? What about *England*?'

'I don't know.'

'What do you mean, you don't know?'

'I don't seem to have an opinion about anything more than once or twice a year at the most, I should say.'

'But what about the Common Market? There's no doubt, the island's got to change.'

Philip sat down and stuck different fingers through the holes in his palette. 'The thing is, the civilization of England *exists*. It's therefore terribly exposed to go-getters. Shall we have an expedition in the car?'

Philip possesses an ancient Peugeot with an open top. It is one of his interests to read Acts of Parliament verbatim; there is a Road Traffic Act that has been on the books for decades and that he thinks to have been poorly framed. It relates to traffic lights. To Philip's mind, the wording of the act in no way covers mechanically operated stop signals. A man of principle about the details of things as well as about chief matters, he has made it his long practice to obey only hand signals. In the case of the ordinary electrically operated traffic light, if it signs 'Stop' he looks to right and left and then proceeds with due politeness across the junction. His licence has never been taken away and no accident has ever happened; many policemen have hauled him up, but his decorousness and his careful recital of the wording of the faulty act have made them let him off with a caution every time.

Philip drove the three of them this evening to Hampstead from Battersea, pointing out spots where they had all had a good time and testing the car's new transmission, which he had put in himself last weekend. 'She's going nicely,' he said.

There were piles of radical pamphlets and Government White Papers in the back of the car, neatly stacked. Pemberton was in the front with plenty of room, but when he looked behind him and saw Nora, crowded, intent on some journal, he rather wanted to be in her seat.

'Nora hasn't got much room. Let me sit there,' he said.

'She likes it in the back,' Philip said, glancing to make sure. 'These beastly sodium lights are quite enough to read by.'

But she's not *listening* to me, thought Pemberton, shut out by their composure.

They stopped at a pub, having negotiated the traffic lights with care and illegality, and Philip said he'd like to tinker with something for a moment. He lay under the back of the car with

112

a spanner. In the pub, Pemberton said to Nora that a friend of theirs called Deborah Metcalfe was in trouble and he thought Nora should spend an evening with her.

'What sort of trouble?'

'She just needs company.'

Pemberton put his arm around her as he saw Philip coming into the pub. 'I was saying that Deborah's low, and Nora said she'd spend the night with her tomorrow,' said Pemberton, watching Nora possessively and meaning Philip to see it. 'We'll drop in on her for a moment or two now. I'll take Nora there in a taxi.' He kept his arm round Nora, but it didn't occur to Philip to be jealous.

'I'll drive you there,' Philip said.

'No, I'd rather take a taxi,' said Pemberton, looking at Nora.

'*You'd* rather?' said Philip to Nora, nodding his own easy agreement. 'I expect you might want to spend the night there tonight, too, but come back if you can.'

The trust between them was grating to Pemberton. But later on, when Pemberton and Nora had indeed dropped in on Deborah and when Philip rang up to suggest 'some splendiferous lunch' instead of the evening tomorrow, Pemberton thought he had managed to disturb.

That night, back in Battersea, while Nora was asleep, Philip woke up as usual at four o'clock and went downstairs to read. When he came up again he spent a long time crouched by the window watching his wife asleep in the light of the street lamps outside. Her hair looked pretty on the sheets. He covered up her shoulders. He found himself speaking aloud to her softly in gibberish, as if he were a groom and she was a horse, well loved. The pipes of the old central-heating system banged away as usual.

Every day now, in pursuit of the cause of the banging, the plumbers came. Two days ago they had put in a dose of some chemical to stop the noise. That morning they arrived at half past seven, having grown attached to the technical problem as well as to the Scropes. They were in the kitchen making themselves a pot of tea when Nora came downstairs.

'I'm pretty sure the bedroom radiator's more stable this morning,' she said in a solemn and comradely way, having a cup of their tea.

'We're narrowing it down,' one of them said as they left for the basement.

'You'd get a more peaceful night at Deborah's than here while it's like this,' Philip said when he came down, after listening to the racket below.

'Not in Notting Hill Gate. Not if there's the usual race riot. But I'd better go, all the same. Do you know, Pemberton said something rather interesting on the way back? He suddenly said about nothing in particular, "I can't always say what I want to say and I can't always contradict what I want to contradict." As if it were an infirmity of his.'

'Perhaps that was what made him muck up everything for himself in the fifties.'

'That's what I thought.' Nora finished making some toast. 'What a tale.'

'*Signifying nothing.*'

'We've missed out *told by an idiot,* which might be what worries Pemberton. I can sometimes see the suspicion that he's a moral idiot weighing on his chest like a millstone. Do you think he *might* be a moral idiot?'

'I think he's in love with you, which shows sense.'

'Oh?' She looked at him. 'Only in his own way, if so. Does it bother you?'

'No, darling. It wouldn't, between us three.'

Deborah had Pemberton and Nora to dinner that night. Pemberton had rung up Deborah to ask her to keep the number to 'the three of us', saying that Philip couldn't come because he had to work.

Deborah lived upstairs in a dilapidated Georgian house in Notting Hill, in a square where some of the most rabid riots were going on. The drawing-room of her flat, which was also where she worked and ate, was furnished with African-print curtains, Victorian leather chairs, and a pretty little prie-dieu with a petit-point back and seat embroidered by her great-grandmother. Her lover, a young black doctor, was home from hospital for a few hours and had their four-year-old child on his knee. There was another friend there, black, called Toussaint, whom Pemberton and Nora knew. Toussaint helped Deborah with the casserole and he and the doctor left soon afterwards, the doctor going back to hospital and Toussaint to a black radical meeting called that day with emergency in the air. Deborah and Nora went out for milk from the slot machine. Pemberton stayed with the child, Freddy.

'He could come with us if you wanted a jaunt,' Deborah had said to them.

'No,' said Pemberton, putting his arm round Nora, who was holding Freddy, and making a wishful family of them.

When the women had gone the beautiful broken-down old house lay in hush. Freddy, who kept late sleeping and waking